# THE FAIRY REBEL

Also by the author:

# The Fairy Rebel

## by LYNNE REID BANKS
### Illustrated by William Geldart

**Doubleday**

NEW YORK   LONDON   TORONTO   SYDNEY   AUCKLAND

Published by Doubleday, a division of
Bantam Doubleday Dell Publishing Group, Inc.,
666 Fifth Avenue, New York, New York 10103

**Doubleday** and the portrayal of an anchor with a dolphin
are trademarks of Doubleday, a division of
Bantam Doubleday Dell Publishing Group, Inc.

Library of Congress Cataloging-in-Publication Data
Reid Banks, Lynne, 1929–
The fairy rebel / by Lynne Reid Banks :
illustrated by William Geldart. —1st ed.
        p.      cm.
Summary: A rebellious fairy named Tiki, already in trouble for
breaking the rule against wearing jeans, risks the further wrath of the
Fairy Queen by trying to fulfill a human's special request for help.
            ISBN 0-385-24483-5
    [1. Fairies—Fiction.]      I. Geldart, Bill, ill.      II. Title.
                    PZ7.R2737Fai    1988
                    [Fic]—dc19
                                    87-28740
                                    CIP
                                    AC

For "Bindi" and her mother.

# CONTENTS

## PART ONE

## PART TWO

# PART ONE

# CHAPTER 1
## *Earthed*

If you happen to go to school just outside London, you might find yourself sitting next to a girl called Bindi. If you do, perhaps you think she is perfectly ordinary. She has brown hair and hazel eyes and is a little bit plump—*not* fat, mind you, just nicely chubby (though she gets teased a lot about it). She looks and dresses and talks the same as anyone else.

But I am going to tell you why she's not really ordinary at all.

The story starts quite a few years ago. To understand it, you have to know a little about her mother and father.

Her father's name is Charlie, and he's a doctor. Not a surgeon, the kind who does operations, but a GP—the kind who comes to visit you when you're ill. Her mother, Jan, is an actress—and not just any old actress. She would never tell you so, but she was once a star.

That was when she was younger. She was small for her age, and very beautiful. She could sing, and dance. She played young girls' parts on the stage, in films and on television. Everyone said she had a wonderful future.

But then something awful happened.

One day she was acting in a television studio when a heavy lamp fell on her. She was in the hospital for a long, long time, and when she came out— although she was still beautiful and still talented— she couldn't walk properly. She had a bad limp.

So she decided she couldn't really act anymore. She couldn't bear people to see her limp and feel sorry for her.

One good thing came out of her accident, though. While she was getting better she met Charlie, and they fell in love and got married. They bought a small house with a lovely garden which had fruit trees in it. Jan loved trees. She also loved sweet things to eat. She loved them too much in a way, because now that she couldn't get much exercise, she began to put on weight. Soon, instead of being slim, she was rather roly-poly. But she still had a lovely voice, and long dark hair, and beautiful eyes.

When Charlie looked into her eyes, he could see a lot of hurt in them. He wished Jan would talk about this, but she never would. She could still act, and she acted being perfectly happy. She could walk quite well enough to look after the little house and do the cooking and mess about in the garden.

Shopping was a problem at first. But Charlie had a talk to one of the local shopkeepers. After that, Jan would ring him up and tell him what she wanted, and later the same day, a boy on a bicycle—with a special metal basket in front—would bring all her shopping to her in a cardboard box. No one ever told Jan where the bicycle came from. Charlie had bought it.

So things went on for a year or two. But then the hurt in Jan's eyes began to get worse. Charlie understood why.

"Stop worrying," he told her. "The accident only damaged your leg. There's no reason on earth why we can't have a baby."

But it seems there was a reason, though nobody could discover what it was.

Another year went by. Now Jan was beginning to cry in the nights when she thought Charlie was asleep. During the days her face was covered with little shadows. And Charlie had to coax her to sing for him, or even talk very much. So of course Charlie also grew sadder and sadder, and the little house and garden and even the fruit trees seemed to get sad and droopy.

One day, Jan was sitting in the garden under a pear tree. There were sweet ripe pears above her head and all round her on the grass, but she hadn't the heart to eat one. She was just sitting there crying, all by herself. And that was where the story of Bindi really begins.

Suddenly Jan felt something settle on her foot. She glanced down through her tears and saw a fairy, sitting on her big toe.

It is a very rare thing indeed for a grown-up to see a fairy. It's pretty rare for a child to see one, though I've heard of a few who say they have. The reason is that although there are fairies of many sorts and sizes flying about outside all the time (though not as many in town as in the country) they are, of course, invisible. As a general rule, they are not only invisible but unfeelable. They have bodies, very small ones, but they are so light that you can't feel them. You can walk through a drift of them and not even know it—most of the time.

*But,* if a fairy, or an elf, lands on a human being— whether on purpose or by accident—then it not only becomes visible, but it has a solid body, and that body has weight. That's why, when this fairy landed on Jan's foot, she felt it at once, though it was very light—about as light as a rather large butterfly resting on her. (She had bare feet at the time. If she'd been wearing socks she probably wouldn't have felt it at all, and then this story would never have happened.)

Jan and the fairy stared at each other. Jan forgot her sadness in amazement, and then in delight. The fairy was such a sweet little thing. She wasn't specially beautiful. Not all fairies are beautiful, any more than all people. This one, just like Jan, was rather fat. She had a round little face and pale pink hair which glistened in the sunlight. Her wings were neither long nor graceful, but rather short and stumpy, and covered with furry stuff like a moth's wings; but they were a lovely color, a sort of pinky lavender. But the most utterly astonishing thing to Jan—apart from her being there at all—was her clothes. She was wearing a full, floaty top which seemed to be made of tiny petals all stuck together. That was quite fairy-like. But her legs were covered with what looked like a minute pair of blue jeans, and these were definitely not fairy-like at all.

It took a long time for Jan to get over her first shock of surprise, and to notice that the fairy was looking very surprised too. She even looked frightened. Jan saw that she was moving her wings as if she wanted to fly away, but she couldn't. So Jan's first words to her were, "Don't be scared—I won't hurt you!"

15

And the fairy stopped frantically beating her furry little wings and said in a shrill, tiny voice:

"Don't hurt me! And don't catch me! It's not fair while I'm earthed." And then she clapped both hands over her mouth. Until she heard those words come out, she hadn't known that she could speak human language. That's another thing about fairies. They have many languages of their own (Fairian, Elfic, Gnomic) but as soon as they land on a human and are real, in the human sense, they can talk to that person.

"What do you mean," asked Jan, "earthed? What's 'earthed'?"

"I—I—" began the fairy. She looked all around, peering into the pear tree's leaves. "It was all that Wijic's fault! We were playing follow-my-zoomer, and he zoomed between your toes, and I had to follow. But I'm too *fat*, and he knew I was. He knew I'd touch! He just knew it! Wait till I catch him— ooooh!" And once again she tried to fly, and couldn't. So she sat down on Jan's big toe and hid her face.

Because her voice was so tiny, Jan had trouble hearing it, so she bent down and took the tiny little figure in her hand. She did it so gently that the fairy hardly noticed that she was being carried up close to Jan's face. She just huddled there with her stumpy wings limp against her back.

"Don't be sad," said Jan softly.

"I can't help it," gulped the fairy. "I've never been earthed before."

"Is being earthed touching the ground?" asked Jan.

"No! We can touch anything but a person," said the fairy. "Oh, why didn't I *listen* when they told me not to go near people? And you're a grown-up, too!" Suddenly she looked at Jan with startled eyes. "Ah, that's it! That's why I can't just fly away. You don't believe in fairies because you're a grown-up! That means I could be earthed forever!"

"Well, I believe what my eyes tell me," said Jan. "And I see you, so of course I believe. There! Can't you fly away now?"

The fairy stood up in Jan's hand and spread her wings and began to fan the air with them. She rose straight up from Jan's hand and at once disappeared.

Jan felt a sting of disappointment.

"Oh, come back for a minute!" she cried. "Don't go yet."

The fairy reappeared on her hand, as if she'd merely jumped into the air and come down again.

"Yes?" she said in her little tinkly voice.

"Can't we talk for a bit? I was feeling so sad and lonely."

"Lonely?" said the fairy. "What's that?"

"Well—not really lonely, of course not," said Jan hastily. "I mean, I've got Charlie, but when he's out —and he has to be out such a lot, looking after people—I've no one to talk to."

The fairy was looking at her curiously.

"What's that wet stuff on your face?" she asked. "It's not raining."

"Tears," said Jan.

"Tears! Oh, do let me taste one," said the fairy eagerly. "Wijic says they've got such a funny taste, not sweet at all!" And she flew up from Jan's hand

17

(vanishing at once, of course). Jan felt a soft little flutter close to her cheek. Then the fairy settled herself again in the cupped palm of Jan's hand. She had that look you probably had the first time you tasted vinegar, and if you can imagine a fairy spitting, that's what she was doing.

"Ugh! Yuk!"

Jan felt a bit insulted.

"Nobody asked you to taste my tears," she said.

"You could have told me how horrid they are! Please pass me a nasturtium."

Jan picked a big orange nasturtium from the flower bed at the foot of the tree, and held it in front of the fairy, who rolled up her tiny sleeve and stretched her hand deep into the flower. Then she brought it out again, and began licking her fingers one by one. Jan realized that she was eating the sweet nectar from the bottom of the flower to take away the taste of tears.

The fairy gave a last big lick to the palm of her hand and said, "That's better," and wiped it dry on her jeans.

"I never imagined a fairy wearing jeans," said Jan.

"We're not supposed to," said the fairy. *"She* hates them."

"Who does?"

*"Her.* Her Majesty," said the fairy in a whisper.

"The Fairy Queen?" asked Jan in awe. "So there really is a—"

"Of course there is! And we do whatever she says. We *love* her," she said rather loudly, adding in a whisper, "but just sometimes a fairy has to do what a fairy wants to do."

18

"And wear what a fairy wants to wear."

"Mmm." She wriggled in her jeans. "They're so comfortable. And smart. Even if Wijic says I am too fat for them." The fairy stood up. "I must go now."

And without another word, she made a little buzzing sound with her wings, fanning them so hard they became a blur, took off from the tips of Jan's fingers and vanished.

# CHAPTER 2
## Petals and Feathers

That evening at supper, after a long silence, Jan said to Charlie, "I saw a fairy today."

Charlie stopped eating and gave her a startled look.

"No you didn't," he said very firmly.

"Yes," she said, just as firmly, "I did."

"Where?" asked Charlie.

"In the garden, under the pear tree."

"And what did it look like?"

Jan described the fairy in great detail. The glistening pink hair and the moth's wings and the blouse made of petals didn't seem to bother Charlie much, but the jeans bothered him. He got up, came round the table and took Jan in his arms.

"Darling," he said, "I think you need a change. I'm due for a holiday at Christmas, but let's not wait. Let's have it now. I'll take you to Scotland."

"I don't want to go to Scotland," said Jan, "thank you."

"Devon, then."

"No, not Devon either. I really don't want to go

away just now. The garden's at its best. It would be a pity to miss it."

Charlie looked at her. He was frowning, but he sat down again and ate his supper.

The next day, as soon as Charlie had left for work, Jan ran into the garden and stood under the pear tree.

"Fairy!" she called.

Nothing happened, but she wasn't altogether surprised. The fairy might be anywhere. Perhaps Wijic or one of the others would go and fetch her. She called softly once or twice more, and then sat down to wait. While she was waiting she fell asleep.

She woke up because something was tickling her nose. It was a tiny feather, wiggling about in the air all by itself. Jan opened her hand and lifted it to the level of her nose. She felt the fairy's tiny, bare feet a split second before she could see her.

"Good morning," Jan said.

"You're not supposed to call me," said the fairy rather crossly.

"Why not?"

"Because you're not supposed to know about me. If the Queen knew I'd let myself get earthed, she'd be very angry."

"I didn't realize."

"What do you want, anyway?"

"Just to talk."

"Haven't you any human friends?"

"Yes, but—"

"But what?"

Jan didn't say anything for a bit, and then said, "My friends are mostly very busy."

21

"So they should be. Everyone should be busy. *We always are.*"

"I'm not."

"Why aren't you?"

"I—I haven't anything to do."

The fairy looked shocked. "We're not allowed to say that," she said primly. "You have to clean your house, don't you? Humans are always fiddling about with their houses."

"I will do it—later, before Charlie comes home. But it's such a bore."

"What's 'a bore'?"

Jan stared at her. It seemed that fairies just didn't know about boredom and loneliness. They didn't have words for them. She realized she knew absolutely nothing about fairies, how they lived or what went on in their heads. She suddenly asked, "Do fairies have houses?"

"Of course. A different one every day."

"You mean, you sleep in flowers and—and—spiders' webs and things."

The fairy gave a shriek of laughter.

"A spider's web! Nobody would try to sleep in a spider's web. You'd stick to it! But flowers . . . yes, if they're big enough. Hollow trees. I like birds' nests best, so lovely and warm."

"And . . . and do you have families?"

"Families?"

"Yes. Mothers and . . . husbands, and brothers and sisters. And . . . and babies."

"Of course we have babies," said the fairy carelessly. "I don't think I know about the other things you said."

"How can there be babies without mothers?"

The fairy shrugged her little fat shoulders. She was lying against Jan's bent fingers with her hands behind her pink, fluffy head.

"Well, how do you get the babies?" asked Jan.

The fairy giggled. "From eggs," she said.

"Like a bird?"

"No." The fairy opened her eyes, sat up and looked round. Then she crawled to the other end of Jan's hand, and beckoned her closer. "It's supposed to be a secret," she said, "but I found out. *She* makes them. The Queen. And when she thinks you're ready, she sends you one. You wake up one day and find it there. Then you have to pretend to think it's just an ordinary egg, and you put it in an acorn cup and take the top off it as if you were going to eat it. Only you take the top off very carefully, of course. And there's the baby, curled up inside! And you have to say, 'Good gracious me, if it isn't a baby!'— as if you hadn't even suspected. That's what *she* likes, so everyone does it to please her. We *love* her," she added, in that strangely loud voice as if she wanted someone to hear.

"Have you got one?"

"Me? No. I'm not ready yet. Please pass me a nasturtium, I'm thirsty."

Jan picked a nasturtium for her. This time the fairy lay on her back, and tipped the nectar down her throat.

"Do you know, I still haven't got rid of that awful taste," she said as she licked the last drop off her lips. "Why do humans make those nasty tears?"

"You nearly made some yourself yesterday," Jan

reminded her, "when you thought you were earthed for good."

The fairy looked up at her—a very odd look.

"That—that awful feeling I had—that was what makes tears?"

"Yes."

There was a long silence while the fairy thought. Then she said, "But what made you make them? What made you have that feeling?"

"I told you. I'm lonely."

The fairy frowned and shook her head. "Tell me in another way."

Jan said quietly, "I want a baby."

"Then your Queen will send you one."

Jan smiled sadly.

"I'm afraid it's not like that with us humans," she said. "Our babies grow inside us. And there seems to be something wrong with me."

"Wrong?"

"I don't seem able to have a baby."

"Oh well, never mind," said the fairy comfortably, and closed her eyes again. But after a while, she opened them. "But you do mind," she said in a different sort of voice, "or you wouldn't have made tears."

"That's right," said Jan.

"Oh," said the fairy.

Jan's hand was getting tired, so she laid it on her knee. The fairy sat for a while, thinking. Then she whirred upward suddenly, vanished, and reappeared sitting on Jan's left shoulder.

"Have you a picture in your head of the kind of baby you'd like, if you could grow one?" she asked.

"Yes."

"Tell me."

"What's the use?"

"You wanted to talk. Talk," said the fairy.

So Jan sighed very deeply, and said:

"I want a girl baby. She doesn't have to be very beautiful or very clever. Just a nice, normal, ordinary baby. I want her to have soft, brown hair like a bird's feathers and skin like rose petals. And eyes like Charlie's, browny-green. And beautiful hands with nails shaped like almonds. And little fat feet."

There was a pause when she'd finished. "How funny," the fairy said. *"I want a thin, thin elf-baby with green hair."* And then she flew away.

# CHAPTER 3

## *The Funny Feeling*

Jan didn't say anything to Charlie this time. Although she didn't like keeping secrets from him she had a funny feeling that she ought to keep this one.

She had a funny feeling altogether.

For one thing, she felt much happier. There was no special reason for this. She stopped crying at night, and in the daytime, too. She limped about the house quite gaily, singing to herself some of her old songs. She was even able to think about dances she had once done without feeling too miserable because she couldn't dance anymore. Suddenly it didn't seem to matter so much.

Jan didn't want to get bored, so she looked in the newspapers and found a job she could do at home. She had to telephone people, and ask them questions and write down their answers. She liked doing this and people were usually pleased when she phoned them. Charlie was very pleased, too, that she seemed so happy.

Soon Jan felt like seeing some friends again. It had been a long, long time since she'd wanted to see any friends. She wouldn't visit them but she asked them to visit her, and they did. She even asked the ones who had babies to bring them. She played with the babies, and the surprising thing was that she didn't feel the least bit sad, even afterward.

"Are you sure you wouldn't like a holiday?" Charlie asked, seeing that Jan was so much better and not miserable any longer.

"Quite sure, thank you," said Jan. "I'm very happy here."

And so she was.

Sometimes, when she wasn't as busy as usual, she would go into the garden and stand under the pear tree. She didn't exactly call the fairy—she didn't want her to get into trouble. But she stood there, just sort of hoping, humming a little tune. She was always rather disappointed when the fairy didn't come, but not sad. She never seemed to be sad these days.

One morning she was sitting by her bedroom window when she felt a feather touch on the back of her hand. She stopped moving at once, and looked. There she was—looking just the same, except that instead of jeans she was wearing a frilly skirt. It made her look like a tiny chrysanthemum, round and petally.

Before Jan could even say hello, the fairy said, "Did you say brown eyes and blue hair, or blue eyes and brown hair?"

Jan blinked. "I didn't say blue anything. I said brown hair and browny-green eyes like Charlie's."

"Oh!" said the fairy. She looked very cross. "What a nuisance!"

"Why?" asked Jan.

"Oh, nothing," said the fairy in a "tossy" little voice and started to buzz her wings.

"Wait a minute!" cried Jan. "Why aren't you wearing your jeans?"

The fairy looked crosser than ever.

"Someone noticed. And told *her*. And she sent me a message. Told me to change. So I had to." She tugged at her skirt. "Look at me—just look! I'm as round as a puffball. I look horrible! Even Wijic says I looked nicer in jeans. *Now* he says they were very slimming."

"Who makes fairies' clothes?" asked Jan.

"Makes them? We do."

"Do you sew them?"

"What's sew? We just *make* them," said the fairy. She looked round in all directions and then beckoned Jan closer. "Watch!" she whispered.

She closed her eyes and drew her hands down herself, back and front. At once the skirt was changed into jeans. The fairy opened her eyes and gave Jan a naughty grin. Then she looked around guiltily and quickly drew her hands up again the other way, and the jeans changed back into the balloony petal-skirt.

"As easy as that?" said Jan. "So why don't you make yourself a lovely slim skirt, or a dress? It's all those bunchy frills that make you look fat."

The fairy seemed puzzled. "I can't," she said. "I haven't got a picture in my head of any other kind of skirt."

"I'll draw you one if you like," said Jan, "or find one in a magazine."

The fairy looked amazed. "Could you really? When?"

"Tomorrow. I'll see you by the pear tree."

"Oh, not tomorrow, I can't. I've got to fix it about . . ." She stopped and looked mysterious. "The next day."

"Right," said Jan. The fairy grinned and buzzed and was gone.

Two days later, Jan took some fashion magazines she'd found and went and sat under the pear tree. It was nearly winter. All the leaves had turned red and fallen off the tree. Jan was wearing a warm cardigan, but she shivered as she sat waiting. What had the fairy meant about brown eyes and *blue hair?* It was worrying her.

She sat there for a long time. The fairy didn't come.

That evening at supper Charlie said, "You're looking sad again."

"No!" said Jan, and smiled brightly. "I'm just a little bit worried, that's all."

"What about?" asked Charlie.

"I don't think you'd believe me if I told you," said Jan.

"Try me," said Charlie, putting down his knife and fork.

Jan looked at him, took a deep breath and said, "Well. You know I told you I'd seen a fairy."

"Oh. That!" said Charlie. "I thought you'd got over all that rubbish."

"Well, I haven't," said Jan. "In fact I saw her again, twice. We had long talks. I told her about . . . you know, how much we wanted a baby, and she . . . she asked me what kind of one we wanted. So I told her. But I think she may have got it wrong."

"Jan," said Charlie impatiently, "what are you talking about?"

"I know it sounds silly," said Jan, "but ever since we had our second talk—I and the fairy, I mean—I've had the oddest feeling that . . . well, that I might be going to have a baby after all."

Charlie's face changed.

"How long ago was it?" he asked.

"Oh, two or three months now."

"Tell me about these feelings you've had, and never mind about the fairy part of it," said Charlie, getting up and fetching his doctor's case.

After a short time Charlie was looking very, very excited.

"I do believe you're right!" he nearly shouted.

That night he made Jan go to bed early. He sat on the edge of her bed, and they talked and talked and talked. Charlie didn't want to hear any more about the fairy, but he did want to talk about the baby, and what they would call it, and where it would sleep, and what they would buy for it, and where they would sent it to school, and all sorts of other things which there was no real need to think about for ages.

And it wasn't for a couple of hours that he remembered that Jan had been worried at supper.

"I've forgotten what you were worried about," he said, just when they were going to sleep.

"Blue hair," said Jan drowsily.

"BLUE HAIR!" shouted Charlie, bouncing up in bed. "What are you talking about?"

"The fairy said something about blue hair. I told her of *course* I hadn't said blue hair, or even blue eyes; I want the baby to have hazel eyes, like yours. But what I keep thinking is, wouldn't it be awful if she'd got it wrong, and the baby had blue hair, or even browny-green?"

Charlie switched on the light, and looked at Jan. He could see she was serious. There was a long silence.

"Not that I believe in her," he said, "but surely a fairy couldn't make a mistake like that."

"She could," said Jan. "Fairies have all sorts of hair colors. *Her* hair is pink."

"But wouldn't a fairy notice that human beings don't have pink and green and blue hair?" said Charlie.

"A lot of young humans do, nowadays," said Jan. "I mean, they dye it funny colors. Anyway she's only a very young fairy. She could easily make a mistake."

"If she's *that* young, I don't see how she could know enough magic to give us any baby at all," muttered Charlie. He turned out the light and lay down. But he couldn't sleep and neither could Jan.

# CHAPTER 4

## *Snow on a Red Rose*

After that, Jan went out into the garden every day and sat for as long as she could under the pear tree. Mild days and frosty days, rain and shine, she went out to give the fairy a chance to meet her. She always hoped she would see the fairy, and when she didn't, she would come back disappointed and worried. She felt more and more sure something was wrong.

Charlie didn't know that she was doing this every day. He would have been cross if he had, because he had told her to keep warm. And he was right. One day Jan sat outdoors too long in a cold winter wind, and caught a very bad cold.

Charlie put her to bed and stayed away from work to look after her.

"Charlie," croaked Jan in her cold-y voice, "do me a favor. Push my bed up against the window so I can look out."

Charlie was worried about drafts but he did as she asked. She propped herself up on lots of pillows and spent the day staring out into the bleak and leafless garden. She didn't feel like eating. Charlie kept popping in to chat with her, but it didn't help.

At night he wanted to move the bed back to its usual place, but Jan wouldn't let him.

"Can we have the window open?" she begged.

"Certainly not," said Charlie firmly. "It's freezing hard outside."

The next morning Jan woke up early. There was a strange grayish light in the room. She sat up quickly and looked out of the window.

"Oh, Charlie, look!" she cried. "Snow! How beautiful! I'd love to go out and play in it," she added.

"Well, I'm afraid you can't," said Charlie sensibly.

When he brought her breakfast, he found her crying.

"What is it, darling? Is your cold worse?" he asked.

"I want to go out in the snow," she sobbed. "I *need* to! Please, Charlie, I'll wrap up very well. My cold is gone—honestly it is!"

Charlie took her temperature and looked at her throat and at last agreed that if she put on two blouses, and two sweaters and warm trousers and fur boots and the thickest scarf and gloves and woolly hat she owned, she might go into the garden for a very few minutes.

At once Jan felt her sadness and sickness leave her. She jumped out of bed and got dressed in all the things Charlie had mentioned, and then she ran out into the snowy garden.

It was lovely out there. The sun was shining, the snow was deep and powdery. She ran about, kicking it up in the air and watching it glitter as it fell in a shower around the toe of her boot. All the twigs and evergreen leaves and even the fir-tree needles had coats of fine snow. Jan even found a rosebush with a red rose on it. The rose was covered with snow, too. Every petal had a rim of snow along its edge.

Roses are summer flowers so Jan was surprised to see it. She picked it. When Charlie called her, she took it to show him.

"Look," she said, holding it out. "Poor, cold little rose."

"It certainly doesn't look very happy," said Charlie, who was at the stove making hot chocolate.

Jan gave the rose a flick to knock the snow off its petals. The snow fell coldly onto her hand, and suddenly something more solid landed in her palm with the snow.

"Oh!" cried Jan, as if she'd been stung. She stood staring into her cupped hand, her mouth and eyes wide open.

"What is it?" asked Charlie, pouring the chocolate into mugs.

"Come and look."

Charlie came and looked.

You never in your life saw a man look more astonished than Charlie did at that moment.

"I don't believe it," he said slowly. "I—do—not—believe it."

A little thing like a red caterpillar was curled in Jan's hand. But it wasn't a caterpillar.

"See?" whispered Jan. "He's earthed, poor little thing." And they both peered closely at the tiny curled-up figure.

He was about the same size as the fairy, but quite

clearly he was an elf. He wore a red tunic and pointed shoes and a pointed red cap. His ears were pointed too, though they were almost too small to see. His hair and his skin were as green as a leaf. He seemed to be asleep.

Charlie was making swallowing noises and screwing up his eyes.

"It's true," he said at last. He seemed quite dazed.

"You don't think he's frozen, do you?" asked Jan suddenly, when the elf didn't move. "He's the same color as the flower. *He* shouldn't be out in winter, either. Oh, Charlie, do make sure he's all right!"

Charlie gave her a funny look. "I'm a people-doctor, not an elf-doctor," he muttered, but he let Jan gently tip the elf into his big hand and had a good look at him. Then he poked him carefully with his little finger to uncurl him.

"He's very cold," he said, "but I believe he's warming up now from the heat of my hand. Let's see if he wakes up by himself."

Jan put a puff of cotton wool over him and after a few minutes she said, "Look, he's moving!" And the next thing was that the elf sat up in Charlie's hand and sneezed. Then he looked around him and saw Jan and Charlie and jumped up in a fright.

"It's all right," said Jan quickly. "I'm Jan, and this is Charlie, and we both believe in you, so you can fly away whenever you like."

The elf had already spread out his wings—two pairs, clear as glass—but then he seemed to relax.

"Jan!" he said. "Oh. It's you. I've seen you with Tiki. I was sitting up in your pear tree that first time you met her."

35

"You must be Wijic!"

"That's me," said Wijic.

"It was because of you that she got earthed on my toe!"

Wijic sniggered unfeelingly.

"Silly thing shouldn't drink so much nectar and get so fat," he said.

"Is she all right?" Jan asked.

"Who? Tiki? How do I know? Haven't seen her for ages."

"Why not?"

"I've been asleep most of the time," said Wijic. "I was having a nap in that rose when the first frost came. I was too cold to creep out, so I just curled up and went back to sleep."

"Wasn't that dangerous? If you're a rose-elf?"

"Who says I'm only a rose-elf? I'm an any-old-flower elf if you want to know. Any *red* flower, that is," he added.

"Can't you change your clothes, like Tiki?"

"Course I can!" said the elf. "I can do anything she can do! Just you watch." And he stood up, kicking the cotton wool aside, and drew his hands down himself. At once his tunic was changed to a red school blazer and red shorts, red knee socks and a red school cap. He looked, for an elf, very odd indeed, and Charlie burst out laughing.

"What's so funny?" Wijic asked in a hurt voice.

"You look like a schoolboy!" said Charlie. "Not an elf at all."

"That's because I wish I *was* a schoolboy and not an elf," said Wijic.

"For heaven's sake, why? If you were a schoolboy, you couldn't do any magic, or make yourself invisible, or anything!"

"Oh—all that's just ordinary. Who needs it?" said Wijic. "Think of the fun of waking up in the morning in a real bed, with real bedclothes, and then having real clothes to put on *one by one,* and then eating breakfast that wasn't all sweet . . . You can't think how sick and tired I am of nectar and honey and all that fairy fruit!"

"But you eat eggs," said Jan, remembering about the acorn cups.

"Only sugar ones," said Wijic. "Human children

37

only have to eat them once a year, but *we* have to eat them all the year round. Chocolate ones and marzipan ones and ones with runny white cream stuff inside . . . Yuk! Once," he went on in a whisper, "I went inside a house—we're not meant *ever* to go indoors, but I did—and I had a nibble of a little boy's boiled egg. It was absolutely the most delicious thing I've ever eaten. But of course, it's not allowed. We're not supposed to get mixed up with humans at all, for fear of getting earthed, or of getting friendly with them."

"Why aren't you allowed to be friendly with humans?"

"Oh, because they're dangerous. They want you to do magic for them all the time, and then things get all mixed up and there can be awful trouble with the Queen."

Jan and Charlie looked at each other.

"Do you mean," asked Charlie slowly, "that if, for example, a fairy like—well, like Tiki, became friends with a human and wanted to do a magic favor for her—er—or him, of course—that might get her into trouble?"

"*Might?* It would," said Wijic. "Without a doubt. You wouldn't catch *me* doing any human a favor, no matter what."

Jan and Charlie looked at each other again.

Then Charlie said, "Listen, Wijic. Would you like a boiled egg now?"

Wijic jumped to his feet, his face, under the school cap, shining.

"Would I!" he cried. "Wow! I mean, I'm already

indoors, so I can't make things any worse if I eat some human food, can I?"

Wijic stayed with them for an hour. Even a caterpillar couldn't have eaten more than he ate. He ate toast and jam, and boiled egg, and peanut butter, and some celery, and a whole pea (a small one), and a good nibble of a chip (cheese and pickle flavor). The funniest thing was that while he was eating all this he was standing on the table, untouched by human hand, so of course they couldn't see him—they could just see the bites of food disappearing and sometimes hear his appreciative grunts, and the crunch, crunch, crunch as he chewed. If they listened very hard, that is.

At last the crunching stopped, and Wijic hopped —or rather, crawled—onto Charlie's hand and became visible again. He was now almost as fat as Tiki.

"Now I know why Tiki eats so much," he gasped. "She *likes* sweet things. I'd be fat if I was a boy and could eat all this lovely not-sweet food." He sank down onto Charlie's hand. "Phew! I can't fly for a while. My wings won't lift me. I think I'll just have a little zizz."

"Wijic," said Jan, leaning over him. "I want you to do me a favor."

"Anything," said Wijic sleepily. "Name it."

"I want you to find out where Tiki is and ask her if . . . if she fixed it."

"Fixed what?"

"The . . . the nuisance."

"Ask her if she fixed the nuisance," mumbled

Wijic. "Okay. No harm in that. Leave it to me."
And he started to snore.

They wrapped him up in the cotton wool and left
him on the kitchen window ledge so he could fly
away when he woke up.

# CHAPTER 5
## *The Queen's Rules*

Three days later, Charlie was taking the rubbish out when Wijic appeared on his shoulder. He'd slimmed down again after his huge meal of forbidden food. He was jumping up and down in a mad sort of way and shouting at Charlie in his thin, high voice.

"What's the matter with you lot? Don't you even put your noses outside when it's a bit cold?"

"What's your trouble?" asked Charlie.

"I've been hanging around here for days waiting for you to come out! I'm freezing! I'm supposed to be a *summer* elf!"

"I come out every morning to go to work," said Charlie.

"Oh. Well, maybe you go out too early. I'm not very good at getting up," said Wijic, calming down a bit. "Anyway, I've got something to tell you, and I have to tell it to you secretly. If the Queen knew . . . !" And he glanced all round him anxiously.

"Come indoors," said Charlie.

"Oh no, I couldn't—"

"We're just going to have some hot buttered toast," said Charlie.

"Oh," said Wijic. "Well. Perhaps just for a moment."

Soon they were all sitting round the kitchen table (except Wijic, who sat on Charlie's hand). Wijic, between bites of toast and grunts of delight, told them his story.

"I flew all over the place looking for Tiki, to give her your message. I went to all her favorite places. There isn't an empty bird's nest for ten miles that I haven't visited. I tried the ring of toadstools where her dancing group meets, her secret hollow tree . . . Where didn't I try! No good. I asked everyone, too. Nobody has seen her for ages."

He stopped to lick the butter off his fingers.

"This yellow stuff is fantastic . . ."

"Go on, Wijic! Never mind the food," cried Jan impatiently.

"Well, in the end I got worried. Lots of summer fairies curl up somewhere snug and sleep all winter, but still, *someone* usually knows where everybody is. The frost fairies leap about a lot, freezing everything, and they generally like playing jokes on the summer fairies, like putting icicles on their noses or freezing their bottoms . . . Anyhow, soon everyone was looking for Tiki. And nobody could find her."

"What could have happened to her?"

Wijic shrugged. "She could have gone south for the winter. Lots of summer fairies do that if they can afford to—"

"Do fairies use money?" asked Charlie.

"What?"

"Money."

"Never heard of that. I meant, if they've saved up enough magic to send themselves abroad. If not, you have to get a swallow to carry you, and they're so selfish they hardly ever will. Anyhow, riding swallow-back is scary, they dive about so much. Tiki's not very brave. Is there anything else to eat?"

Jan opened a small tin of baked beans and gave him one cold. He stuffed his mouth with a great bite and then went on quite cheerfully: "Then of course, she might be dead."

"DEAD!" cried Jan and Charlie together. "Surely fairies can't die," added Jan in horror.

"Of course they die," said Wijic with his mouth full. "What do you think makes all the dust you have to wipe off your furniture? That's dead-fairy dust. If fairies never died, there'd be so many of us you wouldn't be able to move."

There was a silence. Then Charlie said, "But isn't Tiki young?"

"Oh yes," said Wijic, "so am I, but even young fairies die sometimes if they do something silly. Or if they break the rules."

Jan swallowed hard.

"Rules?"

"The rules *she* makes," said Wijic in a lower voice.

"The Queen?"

"Ssssh! Yes. Don't talk about her as if she were just anybody. She makes the rules and if a fairy breaks them, there can be awful trouble."

"Surely she'd never kill a fairy!"

"N-no. No, she wouldn't do that. But she can

take away their invisibility. It comes to the same thing, because then birds, or fish, or cats, or—or—or . . ." He swallowed. "Or some *other creature* usually gets them."

"Your Queen," said Charlie after a long moment, "sounds a bit of a tyrant to me."

"What's that?" asked Wijic uneasily.

"A ruler with too much power and not enough kindness," said Charlie.

Wijic's face turned from leaf-green to whitish green and he dropped the baked bean he was holding. "Oh no!" he said very loudly. "We *love* her. We love the Queen. We all love her, all the time!"

"Oh," said Charlie, surprised, and looked at Jan, whose face had also gone very pale. Wijic grew restless.

"I think I ought to go now," he said.

"But you haven't told us what's going to happen about Tiki," said Jan.

"How do I know what'll happen?" asked Wijic. "Maybe she'll turn up again in the spring. And maybe she won't. All I wanted to say to you is that I couldn't give her your message. Thanks for the food." His wings whirred and he was about to take off when Charlie clapped his other hand down, trapping Wijic between his two hands.

"What are you doing? Let me out!" shouted Wijic from inside the dark cave of Charlie's hands.

"Let him out, Charlie!" cried Jan.

"Do you want a baby with blue hair?" asked Charlie. His face was grim.

Jan sat down very suddenly. She felt sick. Charlie lifted his closed hands level with his face.

"Now listen to me, Wijic," said Charlie sternly. "You must find Tiki."

"How can I?" wailed Wijic from inside the hands.

"If the Queen wanted to punish Tiki for breaking a rule, how else might she do it?"

There was a silence.

"She might . . . she might put her in a wasps' nest," said Wijic in a tiny, scared voice.

"What do you mean?"

"If a fairy is very bad," whispered Wijic, "the Queen sometimes shuts her up in an empty wasps' nest, after taking away her magic. Then she just has to live in all those little dark tunnels, eating scraps of old wasp food—"

"Oh, Charlie!" cried Jan. "Not Tiki! Not for helping us! It would be too awful—I couldn't bear it!"

"For how long?"

"Well, that's the really bad part," said Wijic. "Because sometimes the Queen forgets all about it, and then when spring comes the wasps can come back and open the nest and want to live in it again . . . and *then* . . ."

Jan put her face into her hands with a little cry.

"Oh no! It's too cruel!"

"Wijic," said Charlie, more sternly than ever, "I want you to do us another favor."

"I won't," said Wijic. "I daren't."

"It's more for Tiki. Aren't you her friend?"

After a long time, Wijic said, "Well. What is it?"

"You must go looking for wasps' nests."

"Look for them? Why should I look for them? I know where they are. I know every wasps' nest for miles."

"You do? Why?"

"What a stupid question. If there were a lot of wild tigers living around London, wouldn't you make sure you knew where they lived so as not to go near them?"

Charlie lifted his upper hand a bit. Wijic put his face out.

"Are you scared of wasps then?"

"Scared of wasps? SCARED OF WASPS? Of course I'm scared of wasps. Wasps have special eyes. They can see us. So can bees, but they're not so bad. They're clever. You can reason with a bee. You know, you can say, *I'll* drink from this flower, *you* take that one. Because a bee knows, if he stings you, he's done for too, so he's careful. Wasps are just crazy. They'll chase you and sting you for the fun of it. And one sting, and you're *dust.*"

Charlie stood up, still holding Wijic.

"Wijic. You're going to show us all the wasps' nests you know, and we're going to find out if Tiki is in any one of them."

"Oh no I'm not!" said Wijic—and before Charlie could bring his upper hand down, he had dived straight off into space and disappeared.

# CHAPTER 6
## *The Wasps' Nest*

Neither Charlie nor Jan slept much that night. Charlie walked up and down the room while Jan lay in bed, worrying aloud:

"Poor Tiki! Poor, poor little thing! Shut up alone in the dark waiting for the wasps . . ."

"We don't *know* that. Maybe she's gone abroad for the winter. She could be lying in the sun on some lovely beach for all we know."

"She'd never have gone off and not told me if she'd fixed it about the baby."

"We can't count on a fairy to behave like a responsible grown-up human being. Maybe she just forgot about it. In which case, it's not *poor Tiki*, it's *poor us.*" He stamped up and down the room a few times more and then burst out: "A fairy child with funny-colored hair! It would be better not to have a baby at all."

"Oh, Charlie! But I never asked for one. It was her idea. I'm much more worried about her than about us just now. After all . . ." she said thoughtfully,

47

"we could always dye the baby's hair some ordinary color, even if it was blue or green."

"You did say you wanted her to have pink skin?"

"Yes, oh yes. Like rose petals, I said."

Charlie turned round and stared at her. "Like rose petals!" he said. "What if she thinks you meant an orange rose? Or a dark red one? Or a red and yellow striped one?"

Jan let out a wail and turned her face into the pillow.

Jan's bed was still pushed up against the window. When she woke the next morning, Wijic was astride her arm, kicking her as if her arm were a fat horse.

"Wake up! Wake up!" he was squeaking. "I've found her!"

Jan shook Charlie awake and they both jumped out of bed. "Where?" they cried. "Show us! Quickly!" And they started rushing about trying to get dressed in a hurry; but Wijic was too impatient for that.

He pointed his two forefingers at them and shouted, "Dijiwig!" and they found themselves fully dressed and with their coats on. It was the first bit of actual magic that they'd seen and they both felt rather stunned, but Wijic was appearing and disappearing as he danced up and down on Jan's shoulder, crying, "Come on, come on!" So they hurried out of the house.

It was still very early, and it was a freezing cold, misty morning. No one was about. Wijic grabbed Jan's scarf and flew ahead, pulling at her to follow.

"Where are we going?" Charlie asked, panting after them.

"Not far! Up on the common!"

"Jan can't walk that far. Let's go by car," said Charlie.

Wijic stopped so suddenly that Jan bumped into him.

"Oh yes! Much more fun than flying," he said.

So they got the car out of the garage. Wijic insisted on sitting on Charlie's hand as he steered, and kept shouting, "Wheee! This is great!" every time they turned a corner.

"Is she in a wasps' nest?" asked Jan anxiously.

"Yes."

"How brave of you to find her!"

"Oh," said Wijic, "I didn't find her. I asked a pal of mine, a gnome. Their skins are so thick they don't care about wasps. They don't care about anything much. I had to promise to do something for him . . . Well, never mind that. He got the other gnomes on to it, and at midnight they sent a runner to tell me they'd found her."

They had reached the common by now. It all looked pale, frozen and mysterious. The air was very cold, and the ground was icy. Charlie held Jan's arm carefully as Wijic, holding Jan's scarf so as to stay visible, led them, with wings whirring, to a stunted oak tree in a snowy hollow.

If the Fairy Queen had wanted to make sure Tiki would never be rescued, at least by a human being, she had chosen the right place. The oak tree stood in the middle of masses of blackberry bushes. Their trailing briars, bristling with sharp thorns, spread in all directions. When Charlie and Jan came up to them the highest briars reached their shoulders.

"How are we going to get through this lot?" muttered Charlie.

"We should have brought clippers!" cried Jan in dismay.

"Clippers or no clippers, *you're* not going in there," said Charlie. "Wait here. I'm going to try to push through."

He tried. The briars seemed to have a plan of their own. Their thorns clutched at his coat and scratched at his face. Jan, watching, saw them swaying, reaching for him like thin snakes. There was no wind, so it could only have been some awful magic.

Wijic was crouched on her shoulder.

"Please, Wijic, help him," Jan whispered.

He shook his head.

"You don't understand," he whispered. "If the Queen knew . . . It's bad enough that I brought you here."

Charlie was pushing farther and farther in. Jan could hear him swearing at the briars and letting out little shouts every now and then as a thorn clawed at him or tore his trousers. It seemed to Jan that the opening he had forced through the bushes was closing up behind him.

"He'll be trapped!" she whispered. She felt very frightened suddenly. "Wijic, oh, please! Just a little magic—nothing that would show! Please! Don't you want us to rescue Tiki?"

"Oh—all right," said Wijic, not at all willingly. He shut his eyes and clenched his fists and Jan could see his lips moving slightly. Suddenly Charlie began

to move faster. The rude words stopped. And in another few minutes he'd reached the oak tree.

"I'm through!" he called back. "Now: where's the
nest? Oh! I see it—it's right up at the top of the
tree!"

Jan looked up, and now she could see it too—a
thing like a gray football, stuck among the highest
branches of the leafless oak. It had a lid of snow on
it. Jan shivered when she thought how cold, as well
as frightened, hungry and lonely, Tiki must be.

"Fairies can't be lonely," she reminded herself.
But it didn't comfort her. Tiki didn't have her magic
anymore, so perhaps she had some feelings fairies
don't usually have.

Meanwhile, Charlie was struggling to climb the
tree. He seemed to be having trouble. The tree
wasn't very tall and the branches looked to Jan as if
they would be easy to climb. But every time Charlie
put his foot on one of the lower branches, it slipped
off again.

"Everything's covered with ice," he shouted. "I
can't get a grip." His hands kept slipping, too. Jan
looked down at Wijic, who was now standing up on
her shoulder, watching Charlie.

"That's not ordinary ice," he muttered.

Charlie had just managed to pull himself up onto
the lowest branch. He seemed to have a good grip.
Then suddenly, for no reason, he fell off again.
Luckily he landed on his feet.

"What's wrong with me today?" he said angrily.

"Nothing's wrong with you, mate," muttered
Wijic. "You need a bit of help, that's all." And he

51

pointed both forefingers across the brambles and said, "Biliwiki!" in a high, ordering voice.

There was a cracking noise, and suddenly all the ice and snow broke off the tree and came crashing and tinkling to the ground. A lot of it fell on Charlie's head.

"Hey—!" he said, brushing a big bit of ice, like glass, off his hat. He looked at Jan. "What's going on around here?"

"Tell him to climb. Quick!" Wijic hissed into Jan's ear.

"Climb, Charlie! Get the nest, hurry!" called Jan. She still felt frightened. It was so cold and still now that the noise of the falling ice had stopped—it was as if nothing were alive anywhere except themselves.

Wijic was hugging his own shoulders and jumping up and down.

"I've done it now! She must have heard that!" he cried. "Listen, I can't stop here, I must go. Wish I could ride back in the car, but I daren't wait. G'bye!" And he leapt into the air and was gone before Jan could say a word more to him.

Charlie was near the top of the tree now. He leant along one branch and stretched his right hand up for the nest. As he did it, Jan heard something. It was a very strange noise, a sort of whining hum. It was coming from behind her.

She turned her head and saw something like a small, dark cloud hanging over a clump of trees near the road. As she watched, the cloud grew quickly bigger and bigger. And the whining, humming noise grew louder.

Suddenly, she knew what it was. It couldn't be— not in the middle of winter—but it was. *Wasps.* A huge, deadly swarm of them, sent by the Fairy Queen herself to attack them and stop them rescu- ing her prisoner.

"Charlie!" screamed Jan. "Charlie! Look out!"

He turned in the tree and looked toward where she was pointing. A less brave man would have leapt straight out of the tree and started running. But Charlie didn't. He put his foot one branch higher, reached the nest with his hand, and tore it away from a clinging cluster of twigs.

"Jan! Catch!"

He threw it as hard as he could. It flew through the air across the blackberry bushes. Their snake- like briars swayed upward as if to trap it in its flight, but Charlie had thrown it too high for them to reach. As the shrill, furious buzzing of the wasps drew nearer, Jan made a little jump into the air.

She couldn't jump high because of her lame leg. But it was high enough. She felt the cold, papery thing land safely in her hands. She saw Charlie jump down from the tree and start to push his way back through the clinging, clawing brambles, his arms in front of his face.

Then the wasps were overhead and diving down at them.

Jan didn't waste time trying to run. She tore open the nest, scattering bits of it on the frozen ground, calling all the time, "Tiki! Tiki! Come out, it's me, Jan!"

As the first wasps landed on her head and hands and covered Charlie like a black and yellow cloth,

53

Tiki suddenly appeared between two huge wasps on Jan's fingers and screamed out, "Filimizi! Filimizi!"

Her little voice cut like a sharp silver needle through the heavy, angry buzzing of the wasps. And

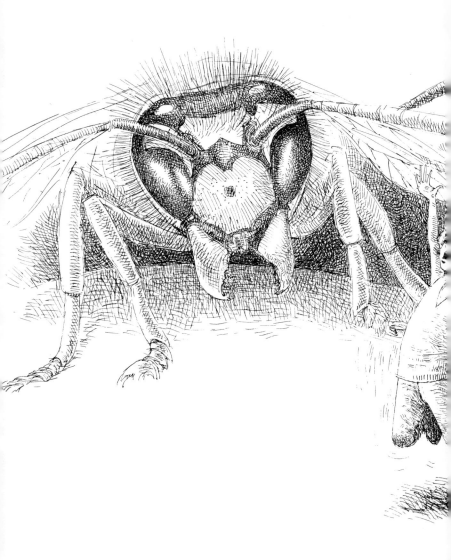

suddenly their noise changed. They didn't vanish or fly away. It was as if they suddenly felt the icy cold for the first time. Their shrill whining turned dull and slow, like the buzzing of a fly after you've

sprayed it with poison. The wasps on Jan's hands, which had been just about to sting her, started to blunder around in circles, and then to fall to the ground. Those still in the air began to fly in circles, too, bumping into each other in a sleepy, drunken sort of way. Some of them dropped and lay on their backs, waving their legs among the frosty blades of grass.

Jan looked fearfully for Charlie. He was standing on her side of the blackberry bushes, looking white and shaken. The black blanket of wasps was falling away from him.

"Charlie, did they sting you? Are you all right?" Jan cried anxiously, hobbling to him as fast as she could.

He put his arms around her.

"I'm okay, what about you?"

"I'm—I'm fine," she said shakily. "Tiki saved us."

They both looked at Tiki, standing on Jan's hand. She looked pretty shaky, too. She was wearing a bright pink tank top, fur-lined boots, stripy leg warmers over her jeans and a woolly hat pulled down over her ears.

"Tiki, what happened?" said Charlie. "How did you do that? I thought you'd lost your magic."

"I didn't use any magic," she said.

"So how did you stop the wasps?"

"Oh, that. All I did was take away the magic that *they* had. Wasps can't fly about in this weather without some magic, you know. It's not natural for them. I just took it away, and the cold did the rest."

"I'm glad to see the Queen let you dress warmly, anyway," said Jan, "before she put you in prison."

"Let me? She didn't let me. Nobody can stop a fairy making her own clothes. About all I had to do in there was to change clothes. What do you think?" she asked, turning round in Jan's hand. "Do you like my new gear?"

"Very smart indeed," said Charlie. "But now let's be getting home. Jan shouldn't be out in this . . ." He looked around uneasily, and Jan knew he didn't just mean the cold.

Putting his arm around Jan, he led her back to the car. On the way, they both looked back toward the oak tree. The thousands of wasps were lying on the white frozen ground, making a dark patch.

"I wonder what the Queen's going to think about *that,*" he said.

"Somehow, I don't think she's going to like it," Jan replied.

# CHAPTER 7
## Sugar Tears

When they were safely home and had taken off their outdoor clothes, they found Tiki had changed, too. Now she was wearing green tights with a pale pink tunic to her knees and round her neck a huge scarf, colored all shades of pink and red, which hung down in front and behind.

"You do look nice," said Jan, admiring her while Charlie made some coffee for them and some hot honey and water for Tiki.

"It was those pictures," said Tiki. "The ones you left out in the garden. I came and had a look at them and put all the pictures into my mind. Since then I have lots of fun changing my clothes. I can even invent new ones now I've got the idea. It's such a shame I've been shut in that awful nest and couldn't show off to anyone."

"But how did it happen that you were put in there? Was it because of me?" asked Jan.

"Yes, of course," said Tiki, but without sounding at all cross about it. "It was because I decided to

58

help you grow a baby." Charlie turned round and stared at her, listening very hard.

"Of course," Tiki added, "I haven't enough magic to do that sort of trick. That's really very hard stuff, you need to save up for ages, not do any little bits of magic, just save and save. Some fairies can save for years to do something big, but somehow I never can . . .

"So what I did, you see, was I borrowed. I went around to everyone I knew, fairies and elves, and gnomes even (though gnomes haven't got much magic: they can't even fly).

"The older fairies did warn me. They said I oughtn't to mix in—that it was none of my business. They even told me the Queen wouldn't like it. She doesn't like us ordinary fairies getting big ideas . . . So after that I pretended I wanted the magic to go south for a holiday.

"I collected all the magic I could. I could feel myself getting stronger and stronger—it was really exciting—and soon I knew I could do it. So I went to the library and found the right words in one of the books, and one night when you were asleep I slipped into your room and said them. I used up all my saved-up magic on you. And that was it. The only trouble was . . ."

"You'd made the hair the wrong color," said Charlie.

"Yes. I'm sorry. I got in a muddle. I remembered about the rose petals—"

"What sort of rose?" asked Jan quickly.

"Oh, pink. I'm really a pink-rose fairy," said Tiki

proudly. "They are the nicest. Besides, I can see you're both pink. I'm not stupid."

"H'm," said Charlie, pouring the coffee. "So what about her hair?"

"Well," said Tiki. "I remembered you'd said 'like a bird's feathers' and I could think of so many really pretty-colored birds, like blue tits and chaffinches and canaries—not to mention parrots—"

"Parrots!"

"Now, don't worry. I see that was silly. Only I'd used up every bit of magic I could lay my hands on, just to get your baby started. To change something after that would have been really tricky. And expensive! I was so worried about it, for fear you wouldn't be pleased, that I—that I—well, there was only one thing I could do."

"What?"

"I . . . I asked the Queen to fix it for me."

Charlie and Jan stared at her. From what they'd heard of the Queen, they found this very surprising.

"You dared to go and see her?"

"Oh no! Not to *see* her. Mere fairies like me never see her. But I got a rather grand master-elf I once met at a party to take her a message."

"Was that wise?" asked Charlie.

"No," said Tiki sadly. "It wasn't."

She sipped her hot drink from the cap off a glue dispenser Jan had found for her to use as a cup.

"And the next thing you knew, you were in that awful nest," said Jan.

Tiki nodded. Suddenly she put the cap down and brought her hands up to her face. Her shoulders jerked up and down.

"Tiki, are you making tears?" asked Jan, bending toward her.

She shook her tiny pink head.

"Yes, you are," said Jan.

Tiki lifted a wet face and sniffed.

"They're not like yours," she hiccupped. "They're sweet ones. I never thought I could make any, though. Fairies aren't supposed to. We never *used* to, before . . ."

"Before what?" asked Jan.

"Just—before," said Tiki with a gulp. "You see, I really did love the Queen. I believed she was good. I trusted her."

She wiped her eyes with the end of her colored scarf.

"It was horrible in there," she said. "All dark and empty and—and—"

"Lonely?"

"Is that what it means? With no friends to talk to?"

"Yes."

"Oh, I'm glad I made your baby start growing!" she said suddenly. "No matter what."

"But what about the hair?" asked Charlie, refilling Tiki's cap-cup with one drop of honey water.

"Well, I'll try to explain," said Tiki. "The Queen took away all the magic I had when she *innesterated* me—"

"Innesterated? You mean, put you in prison?"

"In a nest, yes. I told you, I hardly had any magic left: I'd used it all up on you. But what she can't do is stop me getting more."

"Wait a bit," said Charlie. "You mean, a fairy is always growing more magic?"

"Yes. It just keeps on coming. We can use it or save it up, but it never stops. Like hair. I mean, if *you* were innesterated—"

"Put in prison—"

"Someone might keep cutting your hair short but they couldn't stop it growing."

"And didn't the Queen keep cutting your magic short as it grew?"

Tiki shook her head.

"No. She must have forgotten. She often forgets about fairies she's innesterated. She forgets to let them out in the spring, and sometimes . . ." She dropped her voice.

"Yes, we know," said Jan quickly. "Wijic told us."

Tiki sat up. "You've seen Wijic? *Seen* him?"

"How do you think we found out where you were?"

Tiki sat very straight on Jan's hand. Her eyes grew round and it seemed her glistening hair stood up on end.

"Wijic helped to save me?" she asked at last in an even more tiny voice than usual.

"Yes."

Two more syrupy tears rolled down Tiki's cheeks. Then suddenly she burst out into a tinkly laugh, jumped to her feet, changed like lightning into a pink ballet dress and did a mad little dance all over Jan's hand.

"Tiki," said Charlie. "Would you mind? We need to know about our baby's *hair.*"

"Hair—hair—hair!" cried Tiki, vanishing and

62

reappearing as she jumped about. "I fixed it, I fixed it! Anyway, I *think* I fixed it," she said more seriously, and she changed into jeans and a pink poncho and sat down again.

"As soon as I had saved enough magic—and of course, I had to use a bit of it to magic myself things to eat, after all you can't live on air—I made a tiny hole in the wall of the nest and sent a spell through it to call the grand master-elf. I think he rather fancies me," she said, patting her hair.

"Anyway, he came. I asked him first if he could let me out, and he said no, the Queen would have a fit if he did, and then I told him about you. At first he said he didn't dare do anything and told me off about the baby. But then I said, well, it's done now, and if the baby turns out to have blue hair, everyone will start talking. They'll know it's a fairy child. Think how much better if it looks quite ordinary, then no one need know I was mixed up in it all, and there'll be no bother about it. And do you know what *he* said?"

"No, what?" asked Jan and Charlie together.

"He said," said Tiki slowly, "that a fairy child is a fairy child, and that she could never be ordinary, whatever she looks like."

She looked from Jan to Charlie.

"You never know with fairy children," Tiki went on. "They might *grow magic* like a fairy does, or they might have other special things which only show up later. It was the first time I knew that other fairies have helped humans to have babies, but the master-elf told me it's happened quite often. Have you ever heard of someone called Mo—Mo-something? He could make music."

Jan and Charlie looked at each other.

"Not Mozart?"

"That's the name. Well, *he* was a fairy child. The master-elf knew about it because a foreign elf he'd heard of was the fairy-father of that child—the way I'm the fairy-mother of yours," she said proudly. "I didn't know about fathers and mothers—we don't have them—but the master-elf told me."

"Good grief," murmured Charlie, and put his hand to his forehead. "That's all I need—a genius for a daughter."

"Oh, I don't suppose she'll be that special," said Tiki. "I'm not very special myself. And you said you didn't want her to be very clever."

"I *said* I wanted her to be ordinary and normal!" said Jan.

"Well, you can't have everything," said Tiki in her tossy voice.

"Oh, Tiki—please don't think I'm not grateful," said Jan quickly.

"We both are," said Charlie gruffly.

"Her hair will be brown, anyhow," said Tiki. "I think. The master-elf fixed it. At least, he said he was going to."

"Can we be sure?"

"Sure? What's that?"

"It means *knowing* something is going to happen."

"That's impossible," said Tiki, shaking her fluffy head. "Don't you know the saying, 'Don't count your flowers when they're only buds'? You can never be *sure* of anything."

64

She stood up and stretched. Her furry wings made a sound like *brrrrrr.* "I must go," she said.

"Won't the Queen be angry about you being freed?"

"She probably won't bother. She's so busy."

"She bothered today," said Charlie quietly. "Sending those wasps."

There was an uneasy silence.

"We must hope for the best," said Tiki in her smallest voice.

Then she looked at them both.

"I want to ask you a favor now," she said. "When your egg arrives—I mean, your baby—will you give her a fairy name?"

"Like what?"

"Bindi. That means—expensive, or a treasure. Will you? Because she did cost me a lot. I have to pay back all I borrowed, don't forget! I won't be able to make any fun magic for ages."

Charlie and Jan looked at each other. They nodded.

"It's a sweet name," said Jan.

Tiki gave a little wave. Then she flew up from Jan's hand and vanished.

First Charlie, then Jan, felt a brief flutter against their mouths—a fairy kiss. Fairies kiss by backing up to the person and quivering their wings. But Tiki must have given them a human kiss too, because afterward they both noticed a strange, sweet, scented taste on their lips—the taste of Tiki's tears.

# PART TWO

# CHAPTER 1
## *The Blue Tuft*

One warm evening the following June, Jan strolled all round the garden in her nightgown looking at the rosebushes. She had a feeling the baby might be born the next day, and she thought, "How lovely if only all the roses in the garden were in bloom to welcome her!" But they were all still tight little buds.

Early next morning, Bindi was born. And by eight o'clock, Jan was sitting up in bed with the baby in her arms. Looking out of the window, she saw that the whole garden looked like a sea of pink roses. Every single rose was in flower. The scent came floating up to her bedroom.

To make things even nicer, Charlie rushed down into the garden, chose the most perfect pink rose he could find, and brought it up in a little vase and stood it by Jan's bed.

They were so happy. They looked at every inch of the baby from her toes upward and decided she was exactly what they'd wanted. She had fat little feet, and rose-petal skin, and almond-shaped fingernails, and as for her hair—

"Isn't Tiki clever?" Jan was saying. "She's got everything just right!"

But Charlie, who was holding the baby and gently stroking her little brown-bird's-feather hair, said nothing.

"Is anything the matter, Charlie?" asked Jan, suddenly worried.

"Have you noticed this?" Charlie said quietly.

Jan leant forward and looked. Charlie had lifted some of the baby's hair on the crown of her head. Underneath the brown was a tuft of hair of a different color.

Blue.

It was only a tiny tuft. Perhaps twenty fine hairs in all. Even with the baby's very short hair, you wouldn't have seen it if you hadn't been looking carefully. But it was there all right. Jan and Charlie looked at each other.

"It's her fairy part," whispered Jan. "Should we do anything—dye it perhaps?"

"We could," said Charlie doubtfully, "when she gets a bit older. I don't think dye is very good for babies' hair."

But in the end they didn't bother. As Bindi's hair grew, the blue hairs were easily hidden in the rest of it, and as soon as it was long enough they made a little pony tail with the blue hairs buried in the middle. But that all came much later.

Jan half expected Tiki to turn up and look at the baby—after all, she was Bindi's fairy-mother. But she didn't. Jan might have been worried, as she had been, months ago, after the business with the wasps. But she had had a message from Tiki and Wijic which put her mind at rest, more or less.

The message had come while it was still winter, although the snow had thawed. One morning while Jan was cleaning a window, a robin had landed on the sill. It had something in its beak. It cocked its head at Jan to make sure she was watching, and then dropped whatever it was and flew away.

Jan had picked it up quickly. It was a tiny pink egg. When she touched it to her tongue, she knew at once it came from Tiki, because it was made of sugar. She cracked it open carefully between her front teeth. It was hollow. Out of it fell a little slip of pinkish-brown paper, only it wasn't paper—it was a dried rose petal.

It had some writing on it, but so fine it was impossible to read. Jan ran to fetch Charlie's big magnifying glass from his desk. This is what she read:

We're catching the last swallow
south. Wheeeeeeeeee!
See you!
Tiki and Wiji k

So, as the first months of Bindi's life went by (and of course they were very busy and full months for Jan) she didn't think much about Tiki, and little by

little she almost forgot about her. Or she would have done, but for two things. One was the tuft of blue mixed in with Bindi's brown hair.

The other was the rose—the one Charlie had picked on Bindi's birthday. It was still on Jan's bed-side table. And there it stayed. And stayed. And stayed. Another winter came, and another spring, and the roses were nearly ready to bloom again in the garden. And that rose was still sitting there, as fresh and scented and beautiful as the day Charlie had first picked it.

And then it was time for Bindi's first birthday.

Charlie, who was quite a good cook, baked a cake for her, with some rather lumpy pink icing. Jan wrote BINDI on it in silver balls, and put a candle in a pink holder in the middle. They invited friends and relations to the party, and at the last moment Jan went upstairs to "put her face on" as she called making up. When she came down again she was holding a small vase in her hand.

"Look, Charlie," she said. "It's wilted, finally."

The bedside rose was drooping its head. As she spoke, a shower of petals fell off.

"Never mind," said Charlie. "Time to pick a fresh one," and he went out into the garden.

He came in looking puzzled and excited.

"What is it, Charlie?" asked Jan.

"You're not going to believe this," said Charlie, and held out a rose. At least it looked just like one. But as soon as Jan touched it, she felt at once that it wasn't a rose at all. The stem had no thorns on it—it was smooth, and the petals were stiff.

When the leant over Bindi's cot and put it into

her hand, she gurgled with pleasure, and shook it, and it made exactly the sort of noises babies like best, a mixture of clicks and tonkles and pings and rattles, like all the musical instruments played in school—tambourines, triangles, drums and wood-blocks—all in one.

Jan and Charlie looked at each other across Bindi's cot.

"Of course it's from Tiki," said Jan. "It's her birthday present to Bindi."

"So she's back," said Charlie.

"Why doesn't she show herself?"

"She's probably still having to lie low so as not to let the Queen notice her," said Charlie.

That evening, after the party, Jan went out and put a thank-you present under the pear tree. It was a little silver slipper she had taken off her own charm bracelet, with the smallest pink flower that she could find in it, and the cap-cup full of maple syrup. She picked a pink rose petal and laid it on the grass like a tablecloth and put the presents on it.

Then she stood for a while. She didn't dare call Tiki in case one of the Queen's spies should hear her. Twilight came over the garden. Just when the last light was fading, Jan thought she felt the flutter of furry wings against her cheek and quickly turned to look—but there was nothing there. She sighed and went back indoors.

Next morning, though, the maple syrup had been drunk, and the silver slipper had gone.

# CHAPTER 2
## Rose-Presents

Bindi grew.

On her second birthday, there was a rose with a hollow stem. When Charlie blew up the stem, all the petals filled with air and opened, and soon the rose didn't look anything like a rose—it looked like a balloon, a pink balloon with a funny, surprised face on it.

But it was warmer and softer than a real balloon, and what's more, it didn't burst. It bobbed about on its stem beside Bindi's bed and baby carriage for a whole year, and she played with it and loved it. On her third birthday, it shriveled up.

But there was another rose that year. This one came to pieces. All the petals, which were hard, came out and could be fitted back together again. By the time Bindi was four, she had learnt a lot from that rose. On the eve of her fourth birthday, the puzzle-rose got lost.

But Bindi didn't notice. Because next day, beside her birthday cake, was a new rose with a very long stem. This one had thorns, but they weren't sharp.

75

Bindi soon found out that if you wiggled one, the rose would tell you a story. The stories lasted, at the rate of a new one every week, for a whole year.

On her fifth birthday, the rose was made of some kind of sweet stuff. Bindi, like her mother, loved sweet things, and this rose didn't last a year—it didn't last a day. Every delicious petal was eaten before bedtime on her birthday. Each petal tasted different, and none tasted quite like any kind of candy Bindi had tasted before. The magic thing was that next day the rose was whole again, with a new lot of petals . . . Bindi (and Jan) would have grown very fat indeed that year, if Charlie hadn't been firm. He put the candy away and only brought it out on special occasions.

Bindi's sixth rose had letters painted on every petal. The petals came apart and she could make words with the letters. If she spelt a word wrong, the petal with the right letter on it would jump into the right place. Bindi learnt to spell simple words that year, which got her off to a good start in school.

Just before her seventh birthday she was given a part in a school play. She was to play a queen. Bindi wasn't pleased. Though she was ashamed to say so, she felt she'd rather die than get up on a stage and act.

But then, on her birthday, the rose came. This time it was a big, billowy rose, and when she touched it, she realized that its petals were made of fine, fine silk. She tugged one, and it drew out, and unfolded, and so did all the other petals, until Bindi was surrounded by masses of pale pink silk. Then Jan found a green edge and picked it up and shook

76

all the silk out, and there was the most beautiful pink and green dress—absolutely perfect for the part of the queen.

And the moment Bindi tried it on, and felt the soft, scented silk against her skin, and saw how grown-up and proud she looked in the mirror, the oddest thing happened. All her shyness left her. She felt like a queen. She suddenly couldn't wait to stand up on that stage at school and show them all just how much of a queen she could be.

And she did. She remembered all her lines. And she moved and acted and spoke just like a queen. All the teachers and parents and other children clapped wildly, and Jan and Charlie felt so proud, all they could do was hug each other.

After that, Bindi stopped being shy, and began to love acting. The pink dress went into the dressing-up cupboard and Bindi wore it for dressing up for a whole year. Then it fell into holes.

By now Bindi had begun to look forward to the special rose-present she always got on her birthday. On the eve of her eighth birthday, she and Jan and Charlie tried to guess what sort of wonderful present Tiki would send her this year.

Of course, Jan had told her about Tiki, and Wijic, and the magic beginning to Bindi's life. It was their family secret. Even as a very little girl, Bindi knew that she mustn't boast about it or tell anyone at all, though she often longed to. But she always managed to keep quiet, because Jan had told her that if she talked about them, the fairies might get into trouble.

The only thing they didn't tell her about was the

wasps. They didn't want to frighten her. The odd thing was, it didn't help—she was terrified of wasps anyway.

On the morning of her eighth birthday, the first thing Bindi did was to run down into the garden and hunt about among all the pink roses for the special one which would be her present. She couldn't find it. She touched and smelled every single rose, but they were all quite ordinary. She came back into the house very sadly.

"Mummy, there's no rose-present this year," she said.

"I'll bet there is. Tiki's hidden it, or else you're not looking properly."

"Well, you come and look," said Bindi.

So Jan went down into the garden with her and they both had a good look, but they couldn't find any magic rose. Charlie looked too.

"Oh well," said Charlie, "it couldn't go on forever. Maybe they think you're getting too grown-up for magic."

"But I'm not! I'm not!" cried Bindi, and ran back into the house.

"I hope this doesn't spoil her birthday," said Jan.

"I hope she's not getting a bit spoilt altogether," said Charlie. "She must learn to cope with an occasional disappointment." But he was rather disappointed himself, and so was Jan. At the same time, they were a little bit relieved. They didn't really want Bindi to be a fairy child. They wanted her to be quite normal and ordinary.

So they did everything they could to make it a nice birthday for her, in a normal and ordinary way.

And Bindi enjoyed herself, although she was rather more quiet than usual. In the evening, after her party, when it was nearly bedtime, she went off by herself into the garden.

"She's gone to have a last look," said Jan.

"Hm," said Charlie. He was watching Bindi out of the window. "Yes. She's going from one rosebush to another. Poor little love, it *is* rather sad for her . . . Hey, wait a minute! She's stopped."

Jan came hobbling over to look.

"But that's not a rosebush," she said. "That's that old holly bush that never grows any berries. She won't find a rose on that."

"But she has," said Charlie in a strange voice.

Bindi had had her back turned to the house, and she was bending down. Now she straightened, and turned. In her hand was a rose. But it wasn't like any of the others.

Jan and Charlie hurried out to meet her. She walked up the path to them.

"I've found it," she said, but there was no joy in her voice. "Look."

She held it out to them, and they stood there, the three of them, staring at it.

It was the saddest-looking rose you ever saw. It wasn't pink. It was nearly black. And it wasn't in full flower, like every other rose in the garden. It was only a bud. And it would never open, because it was dying. Its head was hanging limp on its withered stem. Only the thorns looked healthy.

"That can't be it," said Charlie at last. His mouth was dry and his voice was hoarse.

"It must be," said Bindi. She was whispering, for

some reason. "It was growing out of the holly bush. That proves it's magic. But what's the matter with it?"

Jan took it gently in her hand and touched the poor dried-up bud. As she did, the black, unfinished petals dropped away, leaving something like a green star with a yellow center. Something flashed from this yellow part, and Jan, with a little cry, dropped the thorny twig on the path.

"It moved," she whispered. "It twisted in my hand. It—it seemed to burn me for a second, too."

Bindi was reaching down.

"Don't touch it!" ordered Charlie suddenly, catching her hand. "Leave it. It's not your birthday rose, it can't be. Come inside. It's time you were in bed." And he took Bindi's hand in his and walked quickly with her into the house.

# CHAPTER 3
## *The Dried-up Twig*

After they'd tucked Bindi into bed, Jan and Charlie sat up late. At first they just sat looking at each other.

Finally Jan said, "Something terrible's happened."

And Charlie said, "It's none of our business."

Jan felt as if she were married to a stranger.

"How can you possibly say that?"

Charlie turned his face away, and after a few moments he said, in a muffled voice, "I didn't quite mean that."

"I should hope not," said Jan. "Of course it's our business."

"I meant," said Charlie, "that there's nothing we can do. So it doesn't help to worry."

"I'm not so sure about that," said Jan.

Just then the phone rang. It was a patient of Charlie's who said he felt very ill, and could Charlie come? Usually Charlie was fairly cheerful about visiting people at night, but tonight he didn't want to. It was as if he was afraid to leave Jan and Bindi alone in the house.

"Oh, go on, don't be silly!" said Jan. "We'll be all right."

So Charlie went off. And Jan sat for a bit, thinking and worrying. She kept remembering that strange feeling in her hand when she held the dying rosebud. She thought of the twig lying on the path. And then she thought of something else.

Every year, on the night of Bindi's birthday, Jan had gone out into the garden and left Tiki a thank-you present. There were only two charms left on her charm bracelet. One was a little woven silver basket. And one was a tiny silver rose.

She took the silver rose off the chain, found the old glue-cap which had been Tiki's cup, filled it with honey and crept out into the dark garden. She tiptoed across the lawn to the pear tree, keeping well away from the path. The roses on the bushes seemed to glow in the dark. She picked a petal, laid it on the grass and put her presents on it. She was trying hard to make everything seem as it always had in the past.

But as she turned to go back into the house, she caught sight of something that froze her in her tracks. On the path was a weird glowing light. It came and went, never quite going out, like something breathing, alive.

She wanted to run, but she felt she ought not to leave it lying there, any more than you would leave a sharp knife or a bottle of poison lying about. Suddenly she *knew* that everything was not as usual. That *thing* which had stung or burnt her and twisted like something wickedly alive in her hand was deadly dangerous.

Slowly she moved toward it. When she got close, she could see it by its own light. The dead petals lay scattered near it, and the heart of the star beat like a pulse in the darkness.

Jan felt terrified of it. She tried to reach out her hand but as she did, the pulsing light grew stronger, the beat quicker, like a warning signal. Her hand drew back by itself. Her feet began to run before she'd told them to. She found herself back in the house, leaning against the locked back door, panting and gasping.

When Charlie came home, he found her still pale and shaky.

"Charlie, that—that thing Bindi found. We must get rid of it. It's—alive. It's awful."

Charlie saw that she had had a fright.

"I'll see to it in the morning," he said. "Come on. Bed for you." She didn't feel strong enough to argue.

Next morning, Bindi woke up very early. She'd had bad dreams all night, and now she had that flat, let-down feeling you often get on the day after your birthday when all the excitement is over. She had it specially badly this year, because it seemed her fairy had forgotten her.

Then she remembered that there had been a rose-present, even though not a very nice one. She lay in bed thinking how oddly her parents had behaved about that poor, withered rose she'd found growing on the holly bush. They shouldn't have thrown it away. Perhaps it was just one of Tiki's tricks, and if only they'd brought it into the house it would have turned into a magic toy, like the others.

At this thought, Bindi jumped out of bed, put on her slippers and ran into the garden. In the middle of the path, she stopped.

The strange, thorny twig was gone.

Only the dried-up petals still lay scattered on the path. If they hadn't been there, Bindi might have thought she'd dreamt the whole thing.

She turned toward the pear tree. Every year until now, the thank-you presents had gone. This year they were still there. The silver charm rose winked in the grass. Bindi bent to pick it up—and then jumped back.

A big stripy wasp was crouched on the rim of the cap, sucking up the honey.

Bindi stared at the wasp. Somehow it reminded her of a fat tiger, drinking at a jungle pool after it has eaten a big meal.

She felt suddenly sick. And furious. Without stopping to think, she snatched off her slipper and hit at the wasp with it.

"Go away, you hateful thing!" she shouted. "Don't you drink Tiki's honey!"

The wasp flew up with an angry noise. Bindi struck at it again and hit it, but she just knocked it sideways in the air. It buzzed around in a circle and then flew away.

Bindi stood there with one bare foot in the grass and a sick, empty feeling inside her. "I should have killed it," she thought. But she hated killing things.

She walked slowly back into the house. Her parents were still asleep. Bindi decided to get breakfast for herself. She went into the kitchen and opened the cupboard where the cereals were. She chose her favorite, which had the sugar already on it. She got out a bowl, and opened the packet, which was brand-new. First the cardboard, then the sealed paper bag inside. She poured the white sugary flakes into the bowl. Then she dropped the packet on the floor.

Riding on the stream of flakes had come two large wasps.

How could wasps possibly have found their way into a sealed bag?

They were sitting in the bowl on the heap of frosted flakes, feasting on the sugar. They waved their horrid antennae at her and seemed to guzzle. Bindi wanted to shout at them and shoo them away, but she was afraid of them.

She left them there, and ran upstairs to her bedroom. She wanted to jump back into bed and pretend the day hadn't started yet, because so far it had been worse than her bad dreams in the night.

But just as she was going to jump into bed, she stopped.

Lying on her pillow, in the dent where her head had been, was the rose twig.

# CHAPTER 4
## *The Necklace*

She stared at it from a little way away. Well, it certainly was magic, that was for sure. How else could it have arrived here? And if it was magic, it must be from Tiki. Or Wijic, getting up to his tricks. It was babyish to be afraid of a twig.

She reached out her hand and picked it up.

It lay in her hand, a dull, harmless rose stem with the petals gone and just the green leaf-things at the top, like a star, and a yellow pad half hidden among them.

She touched the pad. Some yellow stuff came off on her finger. Pollen. Well. That was natural enough. Maybe it was just an ordinary little twig after all.

She put the twig on her bedside table and got dressed. Then she found that the yellow stuff was still on her finger. She wiped it on the side of her school skirt. It left a long streak that glittered like gold.

She didn't say anything about the twig to her parents. She didn't know why she didn't, she just didn't. When her mother asked why she'd poured out a bowl of cereal and not eaten it, she just said, "I found I wasn't hungry after all."

There was something else she didn't tell them. When she went to the bathroom to clean her teeth, she squeezed a wasp out onto her toothbrush with the paste.

She went to school with her teeth unbrushed.

She was early. She found some of her friends in the playground, and almost as soon as she reached them, one of them, a girl called Manda, said, "What's that hanging out of your pocket?"

Bindi looked down at the side of her skirt. Dangling from her pocket was something that gleamed. She pulled it out. It was heavy in her hand. She held it out, and Manda gasped, and the others crowded round.

"Where on earth did you get *that?* Is it your mother's?"

It was a gold necklace. Most of it was gold. It had some dark brown gemstones in it too. The gold parts were pointed, like little curved knives, or an animal's teeth. Or (but that was silly) like big stings.

"It's not my mother's," said Bindi.

"Did you get it for your birthday?"

Bindi didn't answer. The dark gemstones were shiny. They had a gold stripe across them. They seemed to be staring at her, like round eyes. She hated the necklace—hated it. She wanted to throw it away.

"Put it on, put it on!" the others were saying.

She didn't want to put it on. It was the last thing she wanted to do. But one of the girls snatched it out of her hand and quickly fastened it round her neck.

The moment it was on her, Bindi felt something strange. The necklace seemed to cling to her; the pointy bits stuck into her like little sharp claws, but oddly enough they didn't hurt. She just had the feeling she couldn't take it off again even if she tried.

All the others stood back. They'd gone oddly quiet.

"You should have worn that when you played the queen," said one girl. "It shines, like real jewelry."

"It wouldn't have gone with the pink dress," said Manda. "I think it's ugly. Take it off, Bindi."

Bindi started to put up her hands to take it off, but suddenly she heard a shrill, high voice, not like her own voice at all, saying, "I won't. I like it. It's beautiful. I'm going to wear it always."

All the other children stared at her. Manda, who was her best friend, took a step backward. A boy called Keith, who normally never stopped teasing and bullying her, said, "Well, you'd better button your blouse right up to cover it or Miss Abbott'll make you take it off." And Bindi's hands, which had felt frozen to her sides a minute ago, moved by themselves up to her neck and hid the necklace under her school blouse.

All day at school, Bindi felt the necklace clinging to her. But the warmth of her skin didn't take away its coldness. She couldn't concentrate on schoolwork at all. All she could think of was the necklace. Part of her longed to tear it off and throw it as far away from her as she could. But another part of her couldn't and wouldn't.

She was told off four times during the day for being lazy and not paying attention. She stared at her reading book and couldn't make sense of it. She did her math, but every single sum came out wrong, so wrong that the teacher said she was just being silly. She refused to do P.E. Usually she quite enjoyed it (as long as it wasn't jumping the horse) but today she pretended to be ill and sat out.

The only nice thing that happened all day was that Keith didn't tease her or bully her. In fact he seemed to be trying to make friends with her. She couldn't stand him usually but today she felt different about him. On the other hand, Manda kept away from her.

After school, Bindi walked slowly to the gate. Keith had suggested they meet at the shops. She could see Manda watching. They lived in the same street and they usually went home together, either with Jan or with Manda's mother, whoever came to get them. Today it was Manda's mother. Bindi pretended not to see her and set off toward the shops. She heard footsteps running behind her.

"Bindi!"

She stopped. Manda's mother ran up to her.

"Where do you think you're off to?" she panted.

"I'm not coming home today," Bindi heard herself say. "I'm meeting Mummy."

"Jan didn't say anything to me about that. I think you'd better come with us."

"No," said Bindi. "Mummy told me not to go

home with you. She's waiting for me." And she ran off in the opposite direction from home.

She slowed down when she got round the corner. Her heart was thumping and she felt very strange. Her feet had hardly touched the ground. It was as if . . . as if the necklace had been pulling her along, pulling her almost through the air. She had a funny feeling that if she really needed to, she could fly.

She walked to the shops. She kept trying to think about what she was doing. She had told a complete lie to Manda's mother. As a matter of fact she'd been telling lies all day, to the teachers, to the other children . . . to herself, even. One bit of her mind knew very clearly that the necklace was causing her to behave like this—to change. Another part of her was enjoying it. The two parts of her mind seemed to be fighting each other. It was giving her a head-ache.

At the shops she met Keith. The first thing he did was give her a fruit-and-nut bar.

"Where'd you get it?" Bindi asked.

"Nicked it, didn't I," Keith said, boldly.

Bindi thought, "Yesterday I'd have been shocked. I'd have given it right back to him." Today she wasn't shocked and she ate the chocolate and wished there were more.

"How do you nick things?" she heard herself ask.

"Come on, I'll show you," Keith said.

He led her to the paper shop.

"Aren't you afraid of getting caught?"

"Naaaaa," said Keith.

As they walked into the shop and Bindi saw all the sweets laid out, the necklace was quivering round her neck, digging its spikes into her. It was just as if it were saying, "Go on, go on!" the way you might if you were watching an exciting film.

Bindi's heart was beating. Her hands were trembling. She saw Keith glance round, and then put his schoolbag down on the display of sweets. He dawdled about for a while, and then picked it up again.

"Here! You—boy! None of that—I saw you!"

Keith jumped with fright, dropped the bag, and a Clark bar fell on the floor with it. He started to run away, but the shopkeeper, a very big Sikh with a turban and a fierce-looking rolled black beard, grabbed him.

"You are a thief! I am going to call the police!" he was roaring, as he shook Keith back and forth furiously.

Everyone in the shop took sides. In the end the Sikh let Keith off, because he cried and swore he'd never done it before and would never do it again. But the shopkeeper told him not to come back into the shop, and pushed him out, throwing his schoolbag out after him.

Bindi sneaked out too. She had kept very quiet. She'd also been very busy.

As she and Keith crept off down the road, she passed him the Clark bar she had stolen while all the fuss had been going on. In her schoolbag were two Mars bars, a Snickers and a Heath bar.

# CHAPTER 5
## More Toys!

When Bindi got home, she ran straight up to her room without saying hello to her mother, and tipped out her bag. The stolen chocolate bars tumbled onto her bed with her books.

She looked at them for a moment or two. The points on the necklace stuck into her gleefully, seeming to say: "Go on, go on!" She ate one of the Mars bars. Then half the Snickers. She was full, but the necklace was still urging her on. "More! More!"

"But if I eat the lot, I'll have none left," Bindi said aloud.

Her eyes fell on something lying on the table by her head. It was the rose twig.

Bindi felt no fear of it now. She put out her hand at once and snatched it up. The thorns stuck into her hand, but they didn't hurt. And she knew exactly what she had to do.

Holding the twig like a wand, she tapped it on the Heath bar. In a flash, it became two. She did the same with the others. They doubled themselves. More. More. Another tap—ten bars—twenty!

Bindi felt a wild sense of excitement. She tapped again. The bed was overflowing with chocolate bars. They began to tumble to the floor.

She could do anything with this! She could *have* anything. Anything she liked. She looked round the room. In one corner was her wooden toy-box. She ran across to it and hit the lid with the top of the twig.

"More toys!" she cried. "I want more toys!"

The next second, the lid burst open. Like a volcano erupting, out poured a mass of toys—dolls, stuffed animals, puppets grinning at her, games of every sort and size. They flowed and tumbled onto the floor and piled up around Bindi's feet.

Instead of stopping, Bindi kept hitting out with the twig again and again, and the more she did it, the more toys came. She only paused when a magnificent doll, as big as a real baby, shot up out of the toy-box and landed in her hands. It was oddly dressed in purple satin and gold lace. Its eyes opened as Bindi straightened it. They glowed like green lamps.

An awful feeling went through Bindi. She threw the doll on the bed, but its eyes didn't close. They stayed open, staring at her.

And suddenly she was frightened. All excitement left her. The twig was still clinging to her hand. She felt the necklace throbbing round her neck. She tried to tear it off. Like the thorns of the twig, the sharp gold spikes dug into her. She shook her hand frantically to shake the twig off, but it clung to her. As she shook, it banged again and again on the heap of toys, which were still boiling up out of the box.

Jan was down in the kitchen. She didn't know Bindi had come home. Now, suddenly, she heard her calling. She'd never heard her voice sound like that.

Jan hobbled out of the room and tried to run upstairs. She could hear Bindi screaming, "Mummy, Mummy! Come quickly!" But Jan couldn't come quickly—her lame leg wouldn't let her. She had to go up the stairs one step at a time. It was like the worst kind of bad dream, when you have to run, and you can't.

At last Jan reached Bindi's bedroom door. She tried to throw it open. The handle turned, but something was jamming the door. She cried through the crack, "What is it, love? I'm here!" Bindi was not screaming any words now. She was just screaming. Jan pushed and pushed against the door but she hadn't the strength to open it. She was helpless.

Suddenly she heard footsteps running up the stairs behind her, and there was Charlie. He didn't stop to ask questions. He threw himself against the door with all his weight. There was a crash as the wood split. With a great heave, Charlie pulled the broken door off its hinges.

There was a second's pause. Charlie's and Jan's eyes nearly popped out. Then Charlie jumped back, dragging Jan out of the way.

A torrent of toys, like an avalanche, fell out of Bindi's room. Every kind of toy you can think of. The games came open and the separate parts tumbled everywhere like pebbles among rocks—only the rocks were dolls, and bricks, and trains, and balls, and jump ropes, and puzzles, and computer games. Everything a child might dream of, only it wasn't a dream. It was more like a nightmare, except that it was real. They were real, solid toys. And somewhere in that bedroom which was flooding with toys was Bindi. She wasn't screaming anymore. And Charlie, when he scrambled to his feet, knew at once why she wasn't. She couldn't scream because the toys were burying her.

Like two mad people, Charlie and Jan began to tear at the toy-mountain. They burrowed into it, throwing toys everywhere. All the time they were shouting, "Bindi! Bindi!" Soon they'd dug a kind of cave in the toys, but the toys kept tumbling down on them. They were both bruised from the sharp edges of the boxes of games, the handles of rackets, the wheels of toy trucks, the hard little heads of dolls.

"It's too much!" Charlie ground out between his teeth. "There's too much of it! We can't—"

But Jan wasn't digging and struggling anymore. She had suddenly turned in the breaking-up cave and was half crawling back to the door.

"Keep digging, Charlie!" she cried. 'I'm going to get help!''

She didn't try to run downstairs. She leant on the banister, lifted her feet and slid all the way down on her stomach. She was going to call the police—the fire engine—the ambulance—anything, everything! But when she got downstairs she didn't do that after all. Instead she ran out into the back garden and yelled, "Tiki! Wijic! Help! Help! Help!"

# CHAPTER 6
## *The Tyrant Queen*

Yesterday, on Bindi's birthday, the roses in full bloom had made the garden bright and scented. Now the whole place had gone dark, because they were all dying. The ground was thick with pink petals. All that was left on the bushes were the hearts of the roses, the green and yellow stars. And buzzing thickly around these bare, sad remains were clouds of wasps.

As Jan stood there, staring round in dismay, a wasp left the heart of a dying rose and flew straight at her. It flew against her face, buzzed harshly and swerved away. Like a warning. She turned her head sharply and hit out at it with her hand. Another wasp did the same thing, and then another. The eighth wasp stung her on the cheek.

Jan cried out. But it wasn't because of the pain. It was because she had suddenly understood.

For eight years the wicked Fairy Queen had been biding her time. Or perhaps it had taken her this long to find the child that Tiki had helped to be born. And now she was taking her revenge—she, and the wasps. Jan knew now why the rose twig had not been there this morning when she had gone out to look for it. She even guessed where it was. Bindi had it. It was with Bindi, up there, in her bedroom.

Ignoring the wasps which were now buzzing furiously round her, Jan ran right into the midst of them, down the garden path. Halfway, she turned and looked back up at the house. The window of Bindi's room was blocked with toys. As Jan gazed, there was the crash of glass. The window panes had burst. A shower of glass and toys rained down the wall of the house and smashed on the patio. Only a moment before, Jan had been standing on that spot.

She ran to the bottom of the garden with the wasps buzzing after her. Without stopping to think, she headed for the one thing—the single link she had with the Fairy Queen who was doing all this. The holly bush. She grabbed it with both hands, ignoring the prickles, and shook it, shouting into thin air:

"All right, you Queen! That's enough! Stop it! Stop it now. What more do you want? Do you want to kill us all? Are you so cruel? Do you hear me, Queen of the Fairies? Stop!"

And it stopped. All of it. Everything stopped.

The wasps stopped in midair. Turning her head, Jan saw another shower of toys falling from Bindi's window. They stopped halfway down. Just stopped, as if someone had pinned them to the wall behind them. Everything—the grass, the trees, the rosebushes—seemed to rush away from Jan into a dark mist. There was a deadly, deadly silence in the garden.

Jan was all alone, gripping the holly prickles. She slowly let them go. The bush didn't spring back—it didn't move. Nothing moved. There wasn't a sound, until a high, thin, thrilling voice close to Jan suddenly said:

"Are you speaking to me?"

Jan turned to look.

And there she was. Jan knew at once that this was the Queen.

She was sitting level with Jan's face on a strange brown throne. It took Jan a second to realize it was made entirely of wasps, piled on top of one another, and that it stood on a tall wasp tower.

The Queen was bigger than Tiki. She was about the size of Jan's middle finger. She wore a long dress the colors of oil when it's floating on water—every color there is—glinting and gleaming and ever changing. She wore a glistening crown of wasps' stings.

But it was her wings that fascinated Jan. They were enormous for her size, as dark and gleaming as polished metal, with shaped edges and long sharp points. They moved slowly, like a butterfly's wings when it's resting. Sometimes they were behind her, but sometimes they opened out on each side of her. When they did that, Jan could see a pattern on them, like two big, cold eyes. It was these eyes Jan looked at, not the Queen's real, tiny eyes. When those false eyes were on her, Jan felt frozen. She couldn't speak or move.

"Well?" said the Queen.

Jan tried to speak. She tried to think. Slowly the dark wings folded back. The big eyes weren't look-

ing at her anymore. Jan looked at the Queen's face. She seemed to be smiling coldly.

"Why are you doing all this?" Jan whispered.

"Get down on your knees when you speak to me," hissed the figure on the wasp throne.

Jan tried not to obey, but she couldn't resist. She sank onto her knees. Now the Queen was much higher than her head.

"Look up," she ordered.

Jan looked up. The wings opened, tilted. The eyes pinned her.

"Why am I doing all this?" asked the Queen. "I will tell you why. Eight and three-quarter years ago, a wretched little fairy dared to disobey my commands. She interfered where she had no right to interfere. *She gave life.* Only the Queen may give life. Or take it."

"You haven't killed Tiki!"

The Queen smiled again.

"I do not kill," she said. "It would not be fitting for the Queen to kill."

But she stroked the arms of her throne as she spoke. They moved under her hands. Each arm was a wasp's back. It was as if she stroked pet tigers that would do whatever she ordered.

"Your wasps kill for you," said Jan. "What's the difference?"

The Queen's wings snapped open, the false eyes stared. Jan felt her heart grow cold, her tongue freeze in her mouth. The Queen was not smiling now.

"You have seen a little of my power," she said. "Just a little. What you do not know is that I have turned your dear, good little child—your fairy child, as you dare to call her—into a lazy liar and a greedy thief. What is happening to her up there"—the Queen waved one hand toward the top of the house —"is only the result of theft and of greed. For humans, nothing is ever enough; they are never satisfied. That is why fairies are forbidden to make magic for them or give them gifts. They always want more—more—more!"

"Not Bindi!" cried Jan. "She's not greedy—and she's not a liar—and she's not a thief! Never! I know her, I'll never believe she would do anything really bad!"

"She will do whatever I wish her to do," said the Queen.

"The way you made me kneel to you," whispered Jan.

"What do you mean?" snapped the Queen.

"You forced me to do it. You made it happen. *We* have no magic power. If you used magic to make Bindi do bad things, that's not her fault, it was nothing to do with her! You can't be proud of that, any more than you can be proud that I'm kneeling on the ground!"

The wings opened again but now Jan closed her eyes and would not look at them. She made herself go on:

"You don't think I respect you, do you? You don't think your fairies and elves really love you?"

"How dare you!" The Queen's voice was like the hiss of a snake. "Of course they love me! They say so every day, every hour! They love and respect and

102

honor me. It is my first command that they love me!"

Jan opened her eyes and faced the wings, which were quivering strongly, their awful eyes glaring at her.

"They hate you," she said.

The Queen rose to her feet. Her flowing gown shot gleams of greenish light, like sparks. She quivered all over. The wasps which had been flying in the garden stayed still in the air, but the wasps that made the throne began a low, angry buzzing. The tall pillar they had formed seemed to sway as the wasps crawled over each other.

"They—what?" asked the Queen in a sharp, dangerous voice.

Jan found she could stand, and she did, though awkwardly because of her lame leg. When she stood up she was level with the Queen. She set her teeth and said, "They hate you. They're frightened of you. You let them be killed. You make them cry. You shut them up and then you go away and forget them! They would all be much, much happier if you were—if you were *dust!*"

The Queen stood there on her tall, swaying wasp throne with a look of wild, unbelieving rage on her face.

"Punishment is necessary," she hissed. "I do not forget! And I do not forgive! I will show you something before I punish *you.*"

She raised her arms and clapped her thin hands once above her crowned head.

Her wings opened. They were like the background of a stage. Two wasps—strange flying figures among all the ones still frozen in the air—flew down. They flew close together as if carrying something invisible between them. They settled at the feet of the queen. She pointed a commanding finger, and the next second a fairy appeared between the carrier wasps.

She was a poor, thin, ragged little fairy. Her hair was the pale color of a dead rose petal. She wore a tattered brown dress. Her stumpy wings were shabby and gray, and drooped from her shoulders as if they hadn't been used for flying for a long time. And she was terribly thin. As Jan peered closer, she could just see the white traces on her cheeks, where her sugary tears had dried.

It was Tiki. Changed, half-starved, faded and pitiful, but still, without a shadow of doubt, Tiki.

# CHAPTER 7
## *The Magic Rings*

"Oh," whispered Jan. "Tiki darling. What has she done to you?"

A flicker of a smile crossed poor Tiki's thin, tear-crusted face.

"Nothing much," she said carelessly. "I don't care." And her hands made their old movement, up and down her body, back and front, as if she was trying to change her clothes, to make herself less ragged and pathetic so Jan need not feel so sorry for her. But nothing happened.

So, thought Jan, the Queen, if she really wanted to, *could* stop a fairy changing clothes. She could stop her magic growing. She could fade her natural flower colors and turn her into this poor little creature. And she could stand there smiling at her cruel work.

But Tiki was smiling too. She was not beaten.

"I'm fine," she whispered. "I'm just dressed like this because—because it's winter and the roses are sleeping. And I always get thin in winter because there's no honey."

"But it's summer, Tiki," whispered Jan. "Yester-day was Bindi's birthday."

Tiki looked around her, as if waking up.

"Summer? It can't be. Look at the roses, they're all dead. And if it was Bindi's birthday, I'd have made her a rose-present, wouldn't I? I always make her a rose-present . . ."

She looked fearfully over her shoulder and seemed to see the Queen for the first time. She gave a little cry of terror, dropped to her knees and bur-ied her face in her hands.

"So! You make her magic gifts, do you?" hissed the Queen. "But not this year, eh? This year you had other things to think about than fancy clothes and wasting your magic on human children!"

Once again she reached above her head and clapped her hands, and once again two wasps buzzed down. Jan guessed whom they brought with them this time, and sure enough, when the Queen pointed, Wijic appeared. He, too, was a sorry sight. His red tunic was torn and dirty, his hair had turned brown, his green skin was pale and his shoes and cap were gone.

Yet he, too, when he saw Jan, grinned at her and raised his hand in half a wave. Then he spotted Tiki and his grin slipped.

They stared at each other. Wijic turned for a sec-ond and gave the Queen—standing there so fierce and proud—one look of fury and hate. Then he ran across the backs of the wasps and grabbed Tiki in his arms.

They clung together. Jan couldn't bear it.

"You wicked, cruel creature!" she shouted at the

Queen. "Look at them! Your own fairies! How can you, how can you treat them like this?"

"They disobeyed me, and they are disobeying again!" cried the Queen. "Get back, elf! What do you mean by it? Don't you know that love between fairies is forbidden? You may love only your Queen!" A wasp heaved itself out of the mass under the fairies' feet and thrust itself between Tiki and Wijic. Jan wrung her hands and bit back her tears.

"Now you will see what happens," said the Queen, "when fairies meddle with human beings, and when humans accept their gifts. Look behind you!"

Jan turned. Through the dark mist she could see her house, with the shower of toys halfway down its wall and everything still. At the back of her mind she knew that up there in Bindi's bedroom everything else was still. Time itself was standing still while the Queen sat there on her tower of wasps.

"I am going to call your child," said the Queen.

"No!"

"Yes. I have only to snap my fingers and she dies under the weight of a thousand toys. As for *these* . . ." She pointed her forefingers at Tiki and Wijic. "They are as good as dust already!" Two huge wasps turned their stings upon the fairy and the elf, ready to strike as soon as the Queen ordered it.

The Queen clapped her hands once more.

At once everything started to move again. The dark mist went away. The holly bush snapped back into its place. The wasps that had been flying through the dead roses flew again, though they

107

didn't attack Jan now. The shower of toys fell down the rest of the way with a clatter.

And suddenly, out through the broken window came Bindi.

Jan shrieked with fear. But then she saw that she was sitting on a big blown-up rubber duck. It fell from the window with Bindi on its back, clinging round its neck. The duck bounced as it landed, and Bindi, unhurt, got up quickly.

She looked round and saw Jan at the bottom of the garden.

"Mummy!" she cried, and ran toward her.

Jan wanted to tell her to stop, to go back, but she couldn't say a word. Bindi rushed up to her and clung to her.

"Mummy! It was awful—it was that rose twig—it made everything keep coming and coming . . ."

Jan hugged her close. "It's all right," she said, though it wasn't. There was nothing else she could do.

Then Jan caught sight of Tiki over Bindi's shoulder. She was staring at Bindi's back. A strange thing was happening—unless Jan was imagining it. A little color was creeping back into Tiki's hair, and her wings seemed to be fluffing. She was whispering something—some one word.

Jan leant closer, still holding Bindi tightly. Bindi's ponytail had come loose and her brown hair was hanging down over her shoulders. Tiki was staring at it. And that was what she was whispering, as she had once sung it joyfully while she danced in her pink ballet dress:

"Hair—hair—hair!"

"What are you muttering to yourself, fairy?" demanded the Queen. "It's useless trying to make spells. I've kept your magic well cropped. Nothing can save you now!" And she began to raise her arm.

"Wait!" cried Jan. A strange, a crazy idea had begun to form in her mind. "Don't you—don't you have any—civilized customs?"

The Queen's arm dropped.

"What are you talking about?" she asked coldly.

"Before they die, can't they make a last request?"

"So you think my fairy realm is not civilized," said the Queen. "We are far more civilized than humans!" She turned to Tiki and Wijic. "You may have a last request, both of you, before you are stung to dust."

"I want—I want a hair of Bindi's head," whispered Tiki. And she looked at Wijic and nodded at him.

He looked quite puzzled, but he said, "That's what I want too."

And Jan knew that her crazy idea was right.

"That's not much to ask," she said. "I'm sure your Queen won't refuse. I'll pluck out the hairs myself." And she bent over Bindi, fumbling with her hair.

"Ow!" cried Bindi, and a second later, "Ow!" again.

Then Jan wrapped each hair quickly round her fingertip till it made a ring, and handed one ring to Tiki and one to Wijic.

"Let me look at those hairs," the Queen said suddenly in a suspicious voice. "They are not the same color as—"

But it was too late.

Clinging to the ring of blue hair, Tiki cried out in her piercing little voice:

"Tilidiki! Tilidiki!"

And Wijic, suddenly understanding, waved his blue hair-ring in the air and shouted the same word.

# CHAPTER 8
## *The Great Gathering*

There was one terrible moment when the very air around Jan's head seemed to hold its breath. The Queen's wings snapped forward and the fearsome mask-like eyes glared, and Jan felt Bindi go limp in her arms. Her own blood began to chill in her veins. The Queen's arms rose slowly—her face was twisted with fury—but Tiki and Wijic, with a lightning movement, threw their hair-rings over her arms like lassos, and they seemed to drag, first her arms, and then the Queen herself, down, until she lay crumpled at the foot of her wasp throne.

The tower of wasps seemed to tremble, then totter. Then it began to break up. Tiki and Wijic spread their wings. Tiki was screeching with delight. She was looking pinker every minute. Her hair, standing up on end, was already its normal color, and as her wings beat the air in excitement they seemed to get back all their lavender pink and their furry shine. As for Wijic, he was dancing up and down; he had changed into his favorite schoolboy clothes and was waving his red cap in circles above his head.

As the tall black wasp tower crumbled and broke up, the wasps half flying, half falling, fairy and elf took off, hovering in the air above the ruin.

The Queen crashed five feet to the ground and lay there, the blue hair-rings still circling her arms.

But she was not dust. The wasps' bodies had partly broken her fall. She sat up slowly, trying to shake the rings from her arms. Her wings hung behind her like broken kites, and the eyes on them were hidden.

Jan crouched on the ground with Bindi in her arms. She could hear Charlie shouting somewhere behind her, and guessed that the evil magic toys in Bindi's bedroom had somehow lost their power and that Charlie was free. She called him: "Charlie! We're out here!" And she heard his footsteps pounding toward them.

Then she heard something else.

It wasn't quite hearing. And it wasn't seeing. She sensed it. It was as if the air around her and the ground under her were humming and trembling with the movement of a million pairs of wings and a million pairs of feet. They could not be the wings or feet of the dreaded wasps, because one glance around showed Jan that all the wasps were dead or had escaped. In any case, she felt no fear, but a wonderful feeling of excitement, a thrill all through her as that humming and trembling came closer and closer until she could sense it surrounding her.

Charlie, white-faced, bruised and panting, flung himself onto the grass beside her.

"Jan! Bindi—is she all right? Are *you* all right?"

Bindi was just sitting up, rubbing her eyes and shaking her head.

"What happened?"

"I think you fainted, darling," said Jan. "It's all right now. Just watch."

Sitting there together in the garden, the three of them stared.

At first they couldn't see anything. But Tiki flew onto Bindi's shoulder—Bindi, who had never seen a fairy before, was absolutely pop-eyed at the sight of her—and said, "If you can spare three more of your magic blue hairs, one for each of you, you can see them."

"See what?"

"Something no human has ever seen before."

So there were three more "Ow"s from Bindi as Charlie tweaked three more of her blue hairs out, and they each made a ring round their fingers—and suddenly they could see them.

It was a fantastic sight, never to be forgotten. It was nothing less than a great gathering of fairies, elves and gnomes, coming together to witness the end of the wicked Queen.

The gnomes, who had no wings, marched on the ground—sturdy little people in drab-colored clothes, carrying spades and pitchforks and other tools and implements. They marched in from all sides, and looking farther away, Jan, Charlie and Bindi could see more and more of them—scrambling over the garden fence, or through holes in it, out from under the roots of the fruit trees, digging themselves out of the ground itself. One came out from under Charlie's shoe.

And the air was absolutely thick with fairies and elves. It was like being in the heart of a rainbow. There were all kinds and colors, some with clear wings like dragonflies, some with shaped, brilliant wings like butterflies, and others, like Tiki, with furry moth-like wings. Some of them were beautifully dressed. Others, like Tiki and Wijic, looked tattered and faded, as if they, too, had been in prison or had had their magic taken from them.

The beat of their wings fanned the air. The humans could feel it on their faces as the huge drifts of fairies and elves circled their heads. Some of the fairies hovered in front of them, staring at them, and when they realized that they could be *seen,* they shrieked and shot away with their wings a blur. But Tiki and Wijic flew among them, calling to them in their own language, telling them there was nothing to be afraid of, that Jan and Charlie and Bindi were their friends.

They must have told them, too, that Bindi was a fairy-child, because hundreds of fairies, elves and gnomes began to show an interest in her, flying around her head, touching her with their tiny hands, and lifting her hair to look at the blue hairs. She could hear them chattering in their high voices, and feel their tickling fairy touch.

She didn't wriggle or giggle. She sat quite still, enchanted—knowing, even at the time, how terribly lucky she was to be a part of this very special happening.

But it was not for her that this great crowd of fairy people had come together. The cause was still lying on the ground among the dead wasps with two broken wings.

At last all the gnomes, elves and fairies settled down in a wide, deep circle around the fallen Queen. Many of them perched on Jan, Charlie and Bindi, as if they were grandstands. Charlie found about a thousand fairies sitting on the folds of his shirt, on his arms, his shoulders, even his nose until he politely asked them to move so he could see. Bindi just couldn't believe it when a dozen gnomes scrambled onto each of her shoes and settled down cross-legged along the wrinkles in her socks.

Tiki fluttered to Jan's shoulder and sat down there. She was not wearing her shabby brown dress anymore, but a beautiful pink dress like an Indian sari. Glancing at her, Jan knew she felt the occasion was too solemn for jeans. Or perhaps she'd grown up.

A silence fell. And then the family noticed that standing in the middle beside the fallen Queen was a very tall, handsome elf wearing bright delphinium blue.

"It's my grand master-elf," Tiki whispered to Jan.

The grand master-elf made a long speech in Elfic. Tiki tried to translate, but gave up after a bit.

"Elves love to hear themselves talk," she whispered in Jan's ear. "All it comes to is that with the help of you lot, and Wijic and me, of course, the Queen has lost her power. And would we like to choose a new ruler?" She giggled. "Guess who he's got in mind?"

"It ought to be you and Wijic," whispered Jan.

"Oh no, thanks! Think of the responsibility! No, it's *himself* he means. Look, now he's calling for a vote."

Thousands and thousands of minute hands shot up. Then there was a tiny, but mighty, cheer from the ranks of the watchers.

"Let's just hope he's a good sort who won't abuse his power," said Charlie.

"Do what?" asked Wijic.

"Never mind," said Charlie.

But Bindi had another question, and she spoke it out loudly.

"What's going to happen to the Queen?"

There was a hush over all the fairies.

The Queen was obviously in pain. Despite everything, Jan couldn't help feeling sorry for her.

"Look, Charlie," she said. "Her wings are broken."

"What's going to happen to her?" asked Bindi again.

"Who cares?" said Wijic heartlessly, and there was a murmur of agreement, especially from the gnomes.

"As long as the blue hair-rings are touching her, she can do no harm," said the grand master-elf. All the crowd giggled at the sound of him speaking in human language—it seemed comic to them, somehow.

"Can't she take them off?" asked Bindi.

"No. They cling to her."

"Like that awful necklace clung to me!" said Bindi. And she looked down at her neck. A yellow smear of pollen dust was all that was left of the necklace. She rubbed it off in disgust, and wiped her hand clean on the grass.

"She can't fly, anyway," said the grand master-elf. "Her wings are broken."

Charlie was bending over the Queen, touching her wings with his gentle doctor's fingers.

"It's a simple break in each case," he announced. "I could mend it, I think, if a fairy would help me to fix the splints."

There was another murmur in the crowd. All the fairies, elves and gnomes turned to each other and began to chatter.

"Shall we take another vote?" asked the grand master-elf after they'd talked it over.

This time about a quarter of the crowd was against helping the queen, but the other three quarters voted to help her, as long as when her wings were healed she would be sent to some far-off place and made to stay there and never come back to trouble them.

So some fairies helped Charlie to fix a tiny splint made of a toothpick to each wing and stick it on with little bits of adhesive tape. It may seem strange that they could not just magic her wings better, but none of them was willing to waste any of their magic on her. And her own magic had stopped.

"Won't it grow in again?" asked Jan.

"Not as long as she's wearing the hair-rings," said Tiki. "You don't know just how much power Bindi has in those blue hairs of hers! Hardly any humans have magic powers, but when they do, they are far more powerful than any fairy."

At last all the fairies, elves and gnomes went home (after offering a vote of thanks to Jan and her family). The grand master-elf actually kissed Jan's and Bindi's fingertips in a very courtly way—after all, he was now the Fairy King.

Tiki and Wijic came into the house with the family. Jan made a lovely meal (savory for Wijic, sweet for Tiki, and a bit of both for Bindi). While they ate it, Tiki explained about the blue hairs.

"I don't know if they were an accident, or if the master-elf left them there on purpose," she said. "Anyway, they are very, very powerful, and you can do almost any sort of magic with them that you like. But I must warn you. Once you've used one, it's gone forever, it won't grow again because you're human. Now you've used five. The ones you have left must last you the rest of your life. So be very, very careful, and only pull one out and use it for a really important reason."

Bindi sat looking thoughtful.

"Today," said Tiki solemnly, "you have had a very nasty taste of what can happen if you use magic to get *more.* You see, fairy magic is meant to be good magic, not bad, but when it goes bad, it goes very bad, much worse than the ordinary black magic of bad fairies."

"Are there bad fairies?" asked Charlie.

"Well, the Queen was one, wasn't she?" said Wijic.

"But I mean, lots of them, living together somewhere."

Tiki and Wijic looked at each other across a plate of chips. "I think we'd rather not talk about that," said Tiki. She picked up a small chip and dipped it in some jam.

The fairies stayed for a long time. They seemed quite happy and relaxed. One interesting thing was that they stayed visible even when they weren't earthed.

"It must be because Bindi's one of us," said Wijic. Bindi felt thrilled.

After a while, Charlie said, "I think I'd better go up and look at Bindi's room." They all looked at each other anxiously, and Bindi began to shiver, but when Charlie came back he was smiling.

120

"Everything's back to normal," he reported. "Except the door, of course—I'll have to fix that. And the window."

Then Jan felt brave enough to go up to look. When she came down again, she wasn't smiling at all.

"How can you say it's normal?" she asked Charlie. "The whole room is filthy! There are horrible black greasy marks all over everything, like soot."

Tiki and Wijic looked at each other, and then jumped up. They were both looking much more like their old selves. It seemed their magic must be growing back fast, because they both said, "We'll clean it up, don't you worry." And they flew out through the kitchen door, hand in hand.

"Those two seem to be very fond of each other," said Charlie.

"Maybe now the Queen's lost her power, fairies will be able to fall in love," said Jan.

"And have babies?" asked Bindi.

"Perhaps. It was only the Queen who used to send them in eggs."

Almost at once, Tiki and Wijic flew back.

"It's all nice and clean," said Tiki smugly.

"Already?" said Jan. "You were quick!"

"*And* the door's fixed," added Wijic. "Hadn't enough magic left for the window. Sorry."

"Leave me something to do," said Charlie jokingly.

Jan took the last charm off her bracelet—the little silver basket. In it she put bits of nuts for Wijic. And chips. He liked cheese and pickle flavor best. For Tiki there were crumbs of cake and cookies.

"I wish I had some real candies," said Jan. "A Snickers, for instance. You'd love Snickers, Tiki."

"Don't tempt her," said Wijic. "She'll get fat again easily enough without Snickers." But he was grinning at Tiki.

Tiki was looking rather ashamed.

"There was a Snickers up on Bindi's bed," she said. "I'm afraid I had a bit. Only a nibble! It was *delicious.*"

Charlie looked at Bindi questioningly. He didn't like her eating sweets. To everyone's great surprise, Bindi burst into tears.

"Darling! What on earth's the matter?" asked Jan.

So then of course Bindi told them all about the awful day she'd had at school, and about the necklace and how it had made her change. When she came to the part about stealing the sweets in the shop, Jan turned pale and Charlie's jaw dropped. Bindi expected them to be very angry. If there was one thing they couldn't stand, it was stealing. But instead, Jan took Bindi in her arms and hugged her.

"Poor darling! It wasn't your fault. But we must take the things back and pay for the ones you ate."

Bindi felt as if a great weight had been lifted off her. For the first time that day, she felt really, truly happy.

She was nervous about going up to her room. After what had happened to her there that afternoon, she couldn't believe she could ever feel comfortable in it again.

But Jan and Charlie came with her, and as soon as she stepped inside the room she just *felt* it was all right. Better than that. It felt lovely. Safe. Friendly. Comforting. As if the room had been through a bad time with her and was now more her special place than ever.

She went round it, just touching things. She kept glancing at the toy-box sitting in the corner, looking so ordinary. At last she worked up courage and went over and touched it.

"Open it," said Charlie. "You must make sure that everything is the way it always was before."

Slowly and timidly, Bindi lifted the lid. Nothing happened. She opened it all the way. And then she gave a little gasp.

There was the usual untidy heap of toys, looking just as they had last time she'd put them away. But there was something new. A tiny pink box, the shape of a rose, lying on the furry tummy of her old teddy bear.

Carefully she picked it up. It was the size of her little fingernail. It had a minute fastening, which she could barely open. The lid flew up. Inside, just fitting the rose shape of the box, was yet another rose, made of gold, hanging on a gold chain so fine she almost couldn't see it. She lifted it out.

It was a necklace.

"Your rose-present!" breathed Jan. "Isn't it perfectly beautiful?"

The chain had no clasp. It slipped over Bindi's head. At once the last traces of the awfulness of that other necklace dropped out of Bindi's mind. The little gold rose, warmed by her skin, winked in the sun from the broken window.

"You really are a very lucky girl," said Charlie.

"It's a wonder Tiki had enough magic left to fly, after making that for you."

"Maybe the grand master-elf—I mean the King— lent her some," said Bindi.

"No," said Jan. "I think that was all her own."

"Hers and Wijic's," said Bindi. "I bet they're going to share their magic from now on."

That's almost the end of the story—*that* part of it, anyway.

But I expect you want to know whether the gold rose-necklace could make magic. Well, it could, though none of them realized it for quite a long time. The magic it could do started that very night. I wonder if you can guess what it was. I'll give you a hint.

Bindi was lying in bed, her rose-necklace around her neck, thinking about all her adventures and wriggling excitedly when she thought of others that she might have. After all, she had about fifteen more magic blue hairs! And just as she was planning some wonderful things to do with them, she suddenly sat straight up in bed. She sat there, as still as a rock, for about three minutes. Then, slowly, she lay down again, her heart pounding. She had had a fantastic idea.

She was tired, but she kept herself awake for hours. At last she heard Jan and Charlie going to bed. Still she didn't let herself fall asleep. She lay there, waiting, trembling with excitement.

About an hour passed—a long, long hour for Bindi.

Then she quietly got out of bed and put the lights

on. She unplaited her hair, and pulled it over one shoulder, and sorted through the brown hairs till she found the blue ones. She took one blue hair between finger and thumb, and tweaked it out.

Then, holding it very carefully, she tiptoed out into the passage and into her parents' room.

Her mother was lying, as always, close to the open window. It was a warm night, and she had kicked the comforter aside. One leg—the bad one— was sticking out.

Bindi crept up beside her, bent over and gently twisted the blue hair round Jan's ankle. She kissed her lame foot. She had always loved it, poor foot . . . Now it wouldn't be a poor foot anymore.

She looked at it for a moment in the summer moonlight, and then tucked it under the comforter and went back to bed.

The gold rose round her neck seemed to be dancing.

# ABOUT THE AUTHOR

LYNNE REID BANKS was born in London, England, the daughter of a Scots doctor and an Irish actress. After spending the years of World War II in the Canadian prairies as a child evacuee, she returned to train for the stage at the Royal Academy of Dramatic Art. Five years in the theater as an actress and playwright led to her being the first woman television news reporter in Britain. During this period she wrote her first novel, *The L-Shaped Room,* which was made into a film. In 1962 she emigrated to Israel, where she taught English in a kibbutz, married a sculptor, and had three sons. She returned with her family to England in 1971, and now lives in Dorset and London, but likes to visit the United States every year to tour schools.

Ms. Banks has written more than twenty books, for adults and young readers of all ages from eight upward. Her books for young people include *Sarah and After, The Writing on the Wall, My Darling Villain, The Farthest-Away Mountain,* and *I, Houdini,* a story about a hamster. Her recent book *The Return of the Indian* is a sequel to her popular *Indian in the Cupboard,* which was awarded the 1984 Young Reader's Choice Award of the Pacific Northwest Library Association, and the California Young Reader Medal.